BETTER

NEW YORK TIMES & USA TODAY BESTSELLING AUTHOR
CAREY HEYWOOD

Better

Copyright © 2014 by Carey Heywood

All rights reserved.

Cover Designer: Sarah Hansen, Okay Creations, (www.okaycreations.com)

Editor: Yesenia Vargas

Proofreader and Interior Designer: Jovana Shirley, Unforeseen Editing (www.unforeseenediting.com)

Better is a work of fiction. Names, characters, places, and incidents are either the product of the author's imagination or are used fictitiously. Any resemblance to actual persons, living or dead, events, or locales is entirely coincidental.

ISBN-13: 978-0-9914362-0-0

PRAISE FOR
BETTER

"A heart-wrenching and romantic exploration into the healing powers of love."

—**Renee Carlino**, *USA Today* Bestselling Author of *Sweet Thing*

"This is a real tearjerking, heartstring pulling, emotion-coaster!"

—**Gothic Angel Book Reviews**

"Carey Heywood spins another gratifyingly emotional yarn. A wonderful, moving, and touching tale that will pound your heart and then waltz you around the world and into the heady rush of falling in love. A captivating read that I highly recommend!"

—**Natasha Boyd**, Award-Winning Author of *Eversea*

"Love is too weak of a word for what I feel for this book!"

—**For the Love of Books by J Blog**

"*Better* is a heartbreaking story of loss and sacrifice, a story in a world of emotion all its own."

—**Melissa Collins**, Author of The Love Series

"Carey Heywood is destined for greatness, and I think she has an amazing talent for writing."

—**I Heart Books**

"Better is moving, emotional, and immensely uplifting."

—**J.L. Berg**, Author of The Ready Series

"With *Better*, you get an emotional, romantic, and tearjerking story that's set in the most amazing locations."

—**Nikki Mahood**, Author of The Fallen Series

For Cameron.

CONTENTS

ONE

"Aubrey, that can't be comfortable."

I blink open my eyes and lift my head, wincing as my neck protests the movement. "Nope, I'm good," I lie. "You know me. I can sleep anywhere."

I stand, unfolding myself from the armchair in my aunt's room, our old guest room. Discreetly, I stretch as best I can. "How are you? Can I get you something to drink?" Halfheartedly, I add, "Eat?"

Ally, my aunt, gives me a weak smile. "I'm okay."

"Maybe just some water?" I encourage.

Her appetite, or lack thereof, has been a daily topic of concern over the dinner table. My mom is ignoring it completely. She just shakes her head at my dad and me every time we bring it up. I don't blame her. Ally is her little sister. My mom hasn't given up hope yet that Ally will get better.

I try not to think about it. I feel emotionally wrecked from having my hopes dashed over and over again. Ally just started a new clinical trial that my parents fought so hard to get her into. We all thought that this would be it, her cure. In my opinion, she's sicker now than before she started these new pills. At least before, she would eat.

Ally tilts her head at me. "Maybe later, jelly bean."

I lean over and kiss her forehead, and she slowly lifts her hand to pat my cheek. I feel like crying, but I don't want her to see it, so I mumble something about needing to go downstairs. I pause in the doorway and look back at her.

Six years ago my aunt was diagnosed with leiomyosarcoma. I was seventeen, and I had just gotten accepted to my dream school, Yale. After we found out how sick my aunt was, I opted to stay home and go to the local community college instead. That way, I could help my mom and dad take care of my aunt.

She moved in with us, taking over the guest bedroom. She had just turned forty when she was diagnosed. She didn't look it. I used to raid her closet all the time. She was beautiful and full of this pull that made everyone around her gravitate toward her. It's hard to even recognize her now.

Other than going to see Dr. Julian and using the portable toilet, she stays in bed. Depending on what treatment she's on, she has been both skin and bones to so bloated it looked like she was swelling from an allergic reaction to something.

She notices that I'm lingering in the doorway, so I smile and hurry downstairs.

Once I'm in the kitchen, I pause. Am I even hungry? Or am I just getting a snack because I don't know what else to do right now? I look at the clock. We'll be eating in an hour. I grab a bottle of water and walk into the living room. My dad is at his makeshift desk, mumbling to himself, as he works on his computer. I tilt my head in hello, but he doesn't even notice that I've walked into the room.

He didn't use to be like this, so distracted, but my mom was never good at dealing with paperwork or insurance companies, so my dad has taken on that portion of my aunt's illness. He also still works full time. Before my aunt got sick, my dad was thinking about retiring. Even with good insurance, cancer is not cheap. With all of her medical bills, my dad's retirement has been put off indefinitely.

I sit on the sofa and sip my water.

Minutes later, I jump when my dad says, "Hey, kiddo."

He closes his laptop, stands and comes to sit next to me. "I didn't even see you walk in."

I shrug. "I didn't want to interrupt you."

"How's Ally?"

I shake my head, my eyes stinging. I don't need to say anything. Leaning back, he takes his glasses off and rubs his eyes. I look at him, realizing the last six years have altered all of us.

My father's hair is full gray now. He's thinner, and he always looks tired. I know I look different too. My auburn hair reaches just past my chin. If I had known how long it was going to take to grow back, maybe I wouldn't have shaved it. No, I still would have.

Four years ago, when my aunt's hair started to fall out, we all shaved our heads to support her. My dad's hair came back in gray. There was no change to my mom's hair, which grew quickly, I might add. My hair, on the other hand, took forever to grow back. I also learned the hard way that I do not have a pretty round head. Some people can rock short hair. I am not one of them. My hair also grew back weird. I had to keep getting the back cut while I waited for the top to catch up. It's finally approaching shoulder-length.

My dad puts his glasses back on and stares at the ceiling. He rests his hand on my knee and gives it a squeeze. He's never one to get mushy.

I love my dad. He's always very supportive of me, just in a standoffish kind of way. My mother, on the other hand, is affectionate to a fault. When I was younger, it embarrassed me. Now, I find it comforting.

My dad and I both turn our heads at the sound of the front door opening.

"I got takeout," my mom sings as she heads toward the kitchen.

I inhale through my nose, trying to place what kind of food it is. I'm a picky eater. I always have been. Maybe being an only child made my parents more accepting of my refusal to try new dishes. I do not eat any kind of seafood, fish or otherwise. I also don't eat alfredo sauce, yams (even with marshmallows on top), squash, or cooked fruit. There's probably more stuff that I don't eat, but I can't remember them all.

Whatever Mom got smells like french fries. I can do french fries. My dad and I follow her toward the kitchen. She's pulling plates down to serve our fast food. It seems pointless. All the food she bought came in boxes.

Why dirty plates as well? Maybe I only care because it's my job to clear the table and load the dishwasher. I still have my water bottle, so I sit right down, popping a french fry into my mouth. They're still warm. Yum.

My mom pulls something out of the fridge to make a small plate for my aunt. It's depressing to see the amount of food. I'm pretty sure a Happy Meal serving is three times what my mom has laid out, even considering that it will be a miracle if Ally eats all of it.

Plate in hand, my mom leans down to kiss the top of my head as she walks past. For a moment, her perfume invades the space currently reserved in my nose for french fries. She smells nice though. It's good one of us is holding it together. She probably even showered today. I guess that's what denial will do for you.

"Aubrey, thank you for sitting with Ally while I ran out," my mom says, walking back into the kitchen.

She's brought the plate back down with her, food untouched. She sets the plate on the countertop by the stove. Maybe she plans to try to get Ally to eat again later. She sits down and delicately eats her hamburger, filling us in on her day. She has always had this running commentary. It's like she doesn't know how to be quiet. It's not that it's annoying. I'm used to it. But I'm more like my dad, quiet and reserved.

"Are you going to reenroll for the fall semester?"

I look up at my mom, surprised at her question. "I was going to wait until…" I trail off.

Until what? Ally gets better? Or dies?

I shake my head, unable to finish my sentence, and I focus on my plate. I finish before either of my parents, and I take Ally's plate off the counter to go see if she'll eat anything for me.

When I get to her room, I pause to make sure she isn't sleeping. Sometimes, it's hard to tell.

She is in Stage IV, which means her original tumor has spread from her thigh to her abdomen through her lymph nodes. At one point, she was seeing a holistic healer, who taught her mind healing. Most times, when she's just lying in bed, not sleeping, she's really mentally visualizing herself stripping the cancer away from her lymph nodes and stopping any new tumors. The mind-over-matter technique isn't working, but old habits die hard. I cringe at the expression *die hard*.

I can't tell if she's awake or not, so I turn to leave.

"Aubrey?"

I swing back around. "Hey, Ally. Are you hungry?" I try to seem excited about the organic mush I'm offering her.

She crinkles her nose and shakes her head.

"Ally, you have to eat something." I feel strange lecturing her, remembering all the times she babysat me and fought my picky-eating habits.

Seeing my expression, she relents and nods, but not before she rolls her eyes for good measure.

She could probably feed herself, but her latest tumor is sitting on the bicep of her right arm. It presses uncomfortably if she lifts her arm a lot. For a while, she tried using her left hand, but she ended up wearing her food on more than one occasion. Now, she just lets my mom or me feed her.

She stops me after two bites, sucking her lips into her mouth. I set down the plate and grab a burp tray. She breathes slowly in and out of her nose until her nausea passes. She refuses any more food.

I put the burp tray away and sit down next to her, taking her hand in mine. Her fingers are clammy and swollen.

I've held her hand so many times over her illness. When Ally was first diagnosed, her doctors removed the tumor in her leg. That, along with radiation and chemotherapy, was supposed to cure her. When I hold her hand these days, swollen is the new normal. I'll take swollen forever, as long as it means she's still here.

My mom convinced her to move in while she was on chemo. I stayed home to help when Ally was sick from the chemo. What I remember the most from those days is how focused she was on making sure my mom and I were okay.

She didn't even blink an eye when her hair started falling out. It was my mom's idea for us to all shave our heads. It was that night we started the When I Get Better board. It's a corkboard with pictures of all the places Ally was going to visit when she got better. I glance up at it, still hanging above the dresser. Ally's eyes follow mine, and I cringe, wishing I hadn't even looked at it. Her eyes stay on the board, moving from picture to picture. I clear my throat, hoping to distract her. It doesn't work. Her eyes are transfixed. I give her hand a squeeze and stand, taking her plate with me as I leave her room.

I carry her plate downstairs to the kitchen. My dad is eating a bowl of ice cream at the kitchen table.

"How much did she eat?"

I tilt the plate toward him, and he frowns. I rinse it before putting it in the dishwasher, and then I go to sit next to him. I lean my head on his shoulder. He sets his spoon down and pats my cheek.

"Are you all right, Aubrey?"

I sniffle and shake my head. He puts his arm around me, and I cry. He rests his chin on top of my head and rubs my back until I'm done. When I pull back, he passes me a napkin to dry my eyes and wipe my nose.

"What brought this on, love?"

I take a shaky breath. "The Better board. She was looking at the Better board."

"Ah, that explains it."

"She'll never get to go to any of those places, Dad. We should just take the board down. It's not fair for her to have to look at it."

"We don't know that," he lies. "This new medication might...I don't know, Aubrey. I don't know what to say."

"I don't want her to die, Dad. I just don't want her to die." I lean back into him.

He smells like Old Spice and peppermint. He rubs my back and kisses the side of my head, telling me over and over that it will be all right.

My dad is getting good at lying. My tears stop before I think it's possible. Now, I feel tired.

When I sit back up, I see my dad's neglected bowl of ice cream, and I feel guilty for interrupting him. With everything going on, it's like I've taken a moment of oblivion away from him.

I stand, apologizing. He tries to tell me not to go, but I continue, fleeing back up the stairs and to my room.

I have to pass her room on the way to mine. I walk quickly. I don't want to look inside her doorway. I do anyway, catching a glimpse of my mom sitting with her. Their hands are clasped together, and my mother is leaning in, almost nose-to-nose with her.

I exhale once I'm in my room. All I want to do is sleep. My breakdown in the kitchen zapped whatever energy my afternoon nap had given me. I change into an old T-shirt and some shorts. I collapse onto my bed and will sleep to take me. It doesn't. Instead, I lie there with the image of Ally's eyes as she looked at her Better board burned into me.

I remember when we made it. I was so sure she would get better. Now, I don't know how to act or what to do. My mom is still so sure that this trial medication will work. I know my dad. He's lying when he says he thinks she will get better.

I don't remember falling asleep, but I do remember my dream.

I'm twelve. I have braces and unfortunate skin. Middle school is my least favorite place. A girl, one of the popular ones, tells our class that I'll steal their souls because my hair is red. I try to argue that my hair is auburn, but everyone acts scared of me and runs away.

After riding the bus in a seat all by myself because no one would sit next to me, I'm now home. I don't go inside my house. I just sit on the front porch steps and cry.

I look back when I hear the front door open. Aunt Ally comes and sits down next to me. She's beautiful. She doesn't say anything. She just puts her arm around me and pulls me close.

After I'm fully awake, I go to check on my aunt. She's turned on her left side, facing the chair by her bed. There is a new tumor in her right thigh. Sometimes, it feels better when she's on her side.

I sit and reach out my hand to hold hers. She blinks her eyes open, squinting, before she focuses on my face and gives me a weak smile.

"Morning, jelly bean."

"Hey, how are you feeling?" I squeeze her hand.

11

She grimaces. "Like shit, kid. Let's talk about anything else."

"Um…"

"How's school?"

"Good," I lie. I'm not even currently enrolled.

"Any cute boys?" One side of her mouth pulls up.

Her lips are dry, almost cracked. I reach for her ChapStick on her bedside table and smooth some on her lips.

"I guess."

"Can't be very cute if you're not sure."

I suck at lying to Ally. "You must be right."

TWO

Dr. Julian said the H-word today. My mom has been crying in her room since we got home from Ally's appointment. Ally cried at first, and then she saw how upset my mom looked, so she stopped.

Hospice—her doctor recommended we look into hospice.

It's still undecided as to whether or not Ally will do the next round of pills in the trial. My impression from the doctor was that she should not continue the trial. Ally has been on the pills for three weeks now, and since there is no improvement in her tumor size, the consensus is that the side effect of her loss of appetite is doing more harm than good.

Dr. Julian gave us two timelines—one if she didn't start eating and one if she did. The first timeline was only one month, the second, up to three. Either way, in a calendar quarter, my aunt will be gone.

I don't know what to do. I want to sit with her, but I'm scared I might upset her. I go to sit with her anyway. She's lying down on her side.

Her back is facing the Better board. I want to take it down. I don't want her to have to see it anymore.

My throat is thick when I speak. "Hey, Ally."

"Aw, Aubs. Come sit, sweetheart."

I can't stop the tears streaming down my face now. I sit, and she reaches out her hand. She wants to comfort me. I grip her hand, careful not to squeeze it too hard.

"Everything is going to be okay, jelly bean. I need you to know that. Okay?"

I shake my head, sniffling loudly. "It's not. It's not going to be okay."

She scoots back and pats her bed for me to lie on it with her. I do, facing her, letting her wrap her arm around me. Silent tears run down her face compared to the sobs that rack my body.

When I'm all cried out, she puts her finger under my chin and lifts my head until our eyes meet. She tucks the strands of hair that have fallen forward behind my ear, and she leans forward to kiss my forehead. I close my eyes and drift off to sleep.

At first, when I awake, I think Ally is sleeping. I smile at the peaceful expression on her face.

BETTER

When I reach up to shift her arm, I know she isn't just sleeping.

Dr. Julian was wrong. Ally didn't have a month or three months. She only had one day.

I scramble off her bed. "Mom! Mom!"

My mom runs into Ally's room with my dad a few steps behind her.

"Aubrey, what's—" She doesn't finish her question. She runs to Ally and shakes her. "Ally, honey, Ally. Oh God, Drew help me."

My dad pulls her from Ally. I dumbly stand next to Ally's bed, unable to tell if my mom is crying or screaming.

This isn't right. We were supposed to have more time. Ally wasn't supposed to go like this. I didn't even get a chance to tell her how much I love her, how much I will always love her.

My mom breaks free from my dad's grasp to pull Ally into her arms. My dad leaves my mom and comes around the bed to pull me from Ally's room.

I look up at him. "Why, Dad? Why, Dad?"

He's crying as well. He tucks me under his arm and leads me downstairs to our living room. After opening the liquor cabinet, he pours each of us a shot of something brown. He puts the glass in my hand, and I don't hesitate. I throw it back. I welcome the burn flowing down the back of my throat. I set my glass in front of him, and he pours

15

us each another shot. The burn spreads to a warm feeling in my chest.

My dad slumps into an armchair, shot glass in hand. "I don't know what to do. Do I call the doctor? The hospital?"

He looks so hopeless. I shake my head. I don't know.

Dr. Julian's number is programmed into my mom's cell phone. I go to her purse and pull it out. I feel anger from just looking at his name. He lied to us today. It's only four o'clock. Ally was alive three hours ago. I press the Call button, and then I press the number one to be connected to the front desk of his office. As I wait for someone to answer, I feel the muscles in my throat swell. My body is physically rebelling against having to say out loud that Ally is dead.

A receptionist answers.

"Hello," I croak. "Is Dr. Julian available?" Tears cloud my vision as each word painfully escapes my throat.

My dad watches me with weary eyes as the operator informs me that the doctor is with a patient, and she asks if I would like to leave a message.

"My aunt, Allison Chanthom"—I take a shaky deep breath—"has just died."

I wonder how she was able to understand what I said.

My dad stands to put his arm around me. Ally's death is reason enough to interrupt the doctor's current appointment. I wait for him to come on the line. I wait, and I'm calmer by the time he is on the line.

"Hello."

He lets me know that he is leaving the office to come here to legally pronounce Ally dead. I'm not sure why, but the idea of him being in my home and seeing Ally again makes me furious. I end the call before I explode.

"He's coming here. That liar. In our house. He lied, Dad. He lied."

Even though I'm angry, fresh tears stream down my face. My dad pulls me into a hug before leaving me to go upstairs and deal with my mom.

Again, I don't know what to do. I want to go upstairs and hug and kiss Ally, but the idea of doing that also repulses me.

She's dead. Ally is dead. She's gone.

Her body is there, but her essence has left. I feel like I will regret not hugging her if I don't. I don't want to ever think I could have hugged her one last time but didn't.

My legs feel like lead as I will myself up the stairs. A landing is on the second floor of my house, just at the top of the stairs. My mom is there, sitting on a chair. Her eyes are dead. She does not even notice me as I walk past.

I've heard the expression, *parents should never have to bury a child*. That must be what my mom is experiencing right now. Their mother battled alcoholism, and their father was a traveling salesman. With the difference in ages, my mom practically raised Ally.

I pause in the doorway of Ally's room. My dad is standing in the corner. He is holding his glasses in one hand while his other is wiping his eyes. When he puts his glasses back on, he sees me hovering in the doorway.

I watch him go into dad mode. He straightens his shoulders and walks toward me. He knows what I've come to do, and he is giving me the space to do it. As he passes me, he pauses to kiss my temple.

I take a moment to look at Ally before moving closer. She still just looks like she's sleeping. It seems impossible, but fresh tears sting my eyes. I make no effort to wipe them away. My eyes feel swollen and abused already. I push myself away from the doorway and go to her. I sit in the chair next to her bed. Leaning toward her, I take her hand in mine and rest my forehead against it.

"I'm not ready for you to be gone," I whisper. "I still need you so much." I lift my head to kiss her hand before setting it over her chest. I stand to lie back down next to her.

When we fell asleep earlier, it was her arm draped over me. This time, it is mine over her.

I rest my head on her cool shoulder, hugging her to me. "I love you, Ally. I'll never, ever forget everything you did for me. You were always so much more than just an aunt to me. You were one of my best friends. I just want you to know how much I will always love you."

I cringe when I hear the doorbell. Dr. Julian is here. I squeeze Ally one last time and lift my head to kiss her cheek before standing. I don't want to see him. I blame him for time I—we've lost with her. More than that though, I can't leave her. As much as I want to avoid him, I stay.

I can hear him talking with my father downstairs about arrangements for the body. I want to throw up. She isn't a body. She's Ally.

My father comes upstairs with him. Dr. Julian needs to officially declare her death before she can be moved to the funeral home. Detached, I watch him check her pulse before he writes down her time of death on some form.

Before he leaves, he shakes hands with my father and my mother, telling them he's sorry for their loss. He offers his hand to me. I stare at it, not raising mine, and then he drops his hand and leaves.

The funeral director and another man come to collect Ally. She wanted to be cremated. The concept of being buried made her feel claustrophobic.

There will be a memorial but no actual funeral. She'll stay at the funeral home until the funeral director receives hospital paperwork stating that an autopsy is not needed. Then, my beautiful aunt, my friend, my Ally will be reduced to ash.

Even after they have taken her, my mom and I linger in Ally's room. My brain is playing tricks on me, trying to convince me that she isn't dead but just away. My sight lands on her Better board. I can see her sitting on a beach in the Caribbean, burying her toes in the sand.

There is no mention of dinner that evening. My mom refuses my plea to sleep in Ally's bed that night, calling me morbid. I plod to my room and allow exhaustion to overtake me.

In those blurry moments where I move from sleeping to being awake, I fail to remember what happened. My eyes feel swollen, protesting, as I blink at the light coming in through the window.

In a daze, I walk to the bathroom to freshen up. As I splash water on my face, I remember. I glance in the mirror, and pained hazel eyes stare back at me before I hurry to Ally's room.

Someone has been busy. The linens have been stripped from her bed. The mattress is an exposed reminder that she is gone.

Habits are not easily broken though. There is no hand to clasp. I find myself drifting to the chair by her bed. I'm not sure how long I sit there before the sound of a throat being cleared in the doorway draws my attention.

"Your mom and I are going to go over to the funeral home. They've cleared the cremation. Would you like to come with us?"

I shake my head. I only want to picture Ally here or on that beach with her toes in the sand, not on a pallet rolling into an oven.

My dad walks over to me, his hand brushing over the top of my head. My eyes sting, and I blink until the feeling goes away.

"We'll be back soon, kiddo."

I nod, and he's gone. I can't ignore the empty pit in my stomach any longer. I stand, trailing my fingertips across the stitched edging of the mattress as I walk out of her room.

Downstairs in the kitchen, I stare dumbly into the open fridge, unable to process the concept of preparing a meal. I settle on a bottle of water before checking the pantry for something to eat. After some scavenging, I find a box of chocolate chip granola bars, and I eat two.

After I eat, I run a bath. I stay in the water until it's so cold that I shiver. I'm getting dressed when I hear two car doors shut, signaling my parents' return. My bedroom window overlooks our front yard and driveway. I watch my dad put his arm around my mom's shoulders as he leads her up the front walkway.

I pull on my T-shirt, hurry down the stairs, and open the door for them. This is the first time today I've seen my mom. She reaches her hand out to squeeze mine before my dad leads her upstairs to their room. He comes back down not long after. I'm waiting for him in the living room.

"How was it?"

"I still can't believe she's gone." He takes off his glasses and pinches the bridge of his nose.

"I know." I do.

"Have you eaten anything?" He puts his glasses back on and focuses on me.

"I did."

"Good, good."

I pick at the nail polish on one of my fingers. I can't even remember the last time I painted my nails, but the polish has glitter in it, so I might need a sandblaster to get it all off.

"What happens next?"

He closes his eyes as he spits out a verbal checklist. "The funeral home will call us about her ashes. We need to plan her memorial, but she already told us what she wanted. She has a will we have to handle. I'm really not sure what else."

A chip of nail polish falls on the carpet. "Can I help?"

"With what, sweetheart?"

"Anything."

He nods. "Of course." He sits down next to me, tucking me into his chest. "Of course."

I don't blink away the tears stinging my eyes this time. I let them flow freely down my cheeks, comforted by the smell of peppermint and Old Spice.

For lunch, my dad heats up a can of chicken noodle soup. It feels strange to be eating soup during the summer, but it's nice that my dad wants to take care of me. Having made enough for two, he carries a bowl up to my mom.

Ally's obituary is in the paper today. Before she was accepted into the trial, she had written it herself when things looked bad. She knew what she wanted, even going as far as specifying people send donations to the American Cancer Society in lieu of flowers.

People still send cards and flowers.

Her memorial is going to be on Saturday, and she wanted me to read a poem.

I'm going with my mom to the store today to get a new dress. I need something more conservative than any of the black dresses I currently have. Buying new clothes for a memorial is weird. I'd rather never buy a new dress again and have Ally back instead.

My mom and I grab our handbags and head out. My dad has been taking care of most things since she died. It's a big step for my mom to go out today.

I drive, trying to make small talk with her on the way. She smiles when she would normally laugh, and she nods or shakes her head when she would normally speak when Ally was alive. It's still progress.

My mom slowly walks with me into the department store. After I have an armful of black dresses she sits in a chair by the dressing room. I don't even take the time to show her each dress. I settle on a simple boatneck, cap-sleeve, knee-length cotton dress. I start to pay, but my mom stops me and buys the dress.

She's still quiet as we leave the store, but once we pass the doors and walk into the parking lot, she links her arm through mine.

While we were gone, my dad went to the funeral home to collect Ally's ashes. The lined box holding them is sitting on the coffee table when we get home.

My mom and I both hesitate in the doorway of the living room before walking in. She moves first, approaching the table, reaching her hand out in front of her to trace the rim of the box. Coiling her fingers into a fist, she draws her arm to her chest and hugs herself before hurrying upstairs to her room. That's what she does now when she cries.

She wants to shield her grief from my dad and me, but we both know.

I approach the table, kneeling in front of it. With my hands, I make a circle around the box without touching it. The box is six inches tall, three inches long, and two inches wide by my estimate. All that is left of Ally is in a little box.

If I open the lid and drag my fingers through her ashes, will I feel closer to her soul?

My dad walks into the room. "Find a dress?"

Pulling my hands into my lap, I place one on top of the other and nod.

"How did your mom do?"

"Good. She was quiet but good. When she saw"—I nod toward the box—"she went upstairs."

He rubs his lips together, like he's evening out ChapStick. "I'll go check on her." He pauses in the doorway. "Are you doing okay?"

"It's weird to think she's inside this and that…that all of her fits. Is it heavy?"

"You could pick—"

I cut him off. "I can't, Dad."

He nods. "It is heavier than it looks." Then, he goes upstairs to my mom.

I stand, pausing to let my eyes linger once more on the box before I collect my bag from the foyer, and go upstairs to my room.

My dad closed the door to Ally's room a couple of days ago. I stare at the door as I pass it.

It's almost worse now that it's closed. It makes it easier for me to pretend she's still here.

THREE

Our house is full of people for Ally's memorial. Chairs are set up in our backyard, all facing a table with Ally's urn and a blown-up photo of her from before she was sick.

Sometimes, I forget people other than my mom, dad, and I loved her. Before she got sick, she worked as a teacher for a local preschool. Teachers, parents, friends, and former neighbors come to pay their last respects.

In my new black dress, I hang back from everyone. I do not want their condolences or their excuses as to why they stopped visiting Ally toward the end.

Her pastor, my mom, and I are each going to say something. Her pastor speaks first. He talks about heaven and how death is not really permanent, that she is all around us in our memories of her. When my mom speaks, my dad stands with her, a tender hand resting on her shoulder for support. Though her voice breaks from time to time and she pauses to wipe her eyes more than once, she manages to do it. She tells stories about their childhood and funny things Ally loved. I have to wipe my eyes when she talks about Ally being with her when I was born. How she had always wished Ally would one day have children of her own.

I nervously straighten my dress when it's my turn to speak. Ally's poem is in my hand. I see Dr. Julian sitting in the second row. I glare at him. I still need someone to blame for her death. I am personally on the fence about the whole is-there-a-god question, so I choose to blame him.

I cling to the physical representation of her words, written in her hand, the paper now flimsy from my anxious hands. Before I begin speaking, I rest my hand on top of her urn, hoping she can give me strength.

My voice shakes, but I speak her words, "I've loved my life, but now I sleep, like the setting sun, gentle at its close. This battle lost though I have won. The beauty all around me breathes on. To the ones I cherished, I live on within you. Spend each day with laughter and love. I was tired. I'm now at peace."

After speaking, it is harder for me to hang back. People seek me out to tell me I spoke well or that when they knew my aunt, she always bragged about me. They want me to know how much she loved me. I resent having strangers try to tell me how much my aunt loved me. If they really knew Ally, they would know she told me herself.

I politely nod and smile until all the guests leave. My dad carries her urn back inside, putting it on the mantel. My mom, emotionally exhausted, goes upstairs to lie down. I stay in the backyard, swinging slowly on the tree swing.

What now? I'm not sure what I should do next. It feels like I'm on hold. If I want to enroll for the fall semester, I have to do it soon. I might have already missed the cutoff. I don't know if that's what I want anymore. I look up into the tree, my toe tips dragging through the grass.

Long ago, my dream was to go to Yale. I wanted an adventure, and New Haven, Connecticut felt so far away from Sacramento. So much has changed since then. Now, the idea of being so far from home scares me.

I look down at the ground as the feeling of vertigo comes over me, the sway of the swing aggravating it. I lean forward, reaching out with my hands, until I am on my hands and knees in the grass in front of the swing. I pant until the dizzy feeling passes before I stand back up and head inside, brushing dirt from my knees.

My dad is on the phone. He walks from one room to another as he speaks. I hear bits of his conversation.

"Of course. Monday. Good." He walks by, still talking. "I don't..." He trails off. "Read it."

I sit in the living room, flipping absentmindedly through a cooking magazine. When he hangs up, he comes and sits at his desk.

"That was our lawyer. He's coming Monday to read Ally's will."

I look up. "Her will?"

He nods.

"But I thought…it's not like there's anything left."

He shrugs. "I'm not sure, sweetie. I don't have a copy of her will."

No one makes dinner that night. My dad and I just nibble on leftovers from the memorial. My mom stays upstairs, and my dad takes her a plate.

When he comes back downstairs, I ask him how she is.

"It's been a rough day. Ask me tomorrow."

He turns on the TV. There's a marathon of *The Big Bang Theory* on. I laugh at something Sheldon says, and I immediately feel guilty. Ally has been gone for less than a week. How is it even possible for me to laugh?

I excuse myself and go upstairs to my room. I pause when I pass Ally's room. Instead of continuing on to my room, I gingerly open her door and walk inside, closing it behind me. I rest there for a spell with my back pressed against the door and my hand still on the knob.

With the exception of the bare bed, it still looks and smells the same. Ally loved the smell of vanilla. There are candles and scent sprays on top of her dresser. Her favorite cardigan hangs from the corner of her headboard.

Feeling a chill, I pluck it from its perch and put it on. I curl up on her bed and cry. Slowly, I begin talking to Ally as if she were there. I'm careful not to speak too loudly because I don't want anyone to hear me.

I tell her how angry I am at Dr. Julian and how uncertain I am with what I should do with my life. I bathe, I dress, I feed myself, and I talk with my parents on a daily basis. I have no desire to do anything more than that. Will I always feel this way? I feel guilt from not knowing what to do about school. I know I'm currently incapable of absorbing anything school-related.

I can imagine myself never leaving our house again. I get that it seems extreme and probably not normal. It still doesn't seem real. I spent the last six years certain that she was going to get better. Then, the day the doctor told us otherwise, she died.

I had no time to mentally prepare for the difference. I'm sure people who have lost their loved ones in an unexpected way feel the same way, only not. They are just living their lives like normal until it happens, and then it's a shock to their systems.

I have forgotten what normal is. I do not know how to live anymore in a world where Ally isn't fighting.

At some point, I drift off only to awake in a dark room, unable to remember where I am. Since my room faces the street, there is always a trickle of light that makes its way past the seams of my wooden blinds. There is no filtered glow from our lamppost in Ally's room.

I'm cold, my legs are bare, and Ally's cardigan—while on the long side—does not make a good blanket. I go to my own room and change into sweats and a T-shirt, pulling Ally's cardigan back on before I crawl into bed. The glow from the lamppost is a comforting nightlight to aid my return to sleep.

I'm uncomfortably warm when I wake up, still wearing Ally's cardigan. I shrug it off only to then feel chilled, and I put it back on, hugging myself. I've slept in. It's past ten.

On my way to the stairs, I peek in my parents' room, wanting to see if my mom has gotten out of bed. Seeing the bed is empty and made, I head toward the kitchen. I pass the living and dining rooms on the way. Both are empty. Now in an equally empty kitchen, I wonder where my parents are. It's then that I hear voices from our back deck.

"She needs to go back to school." My dad seems annoyed.

I pause at the back door now that I know they're talking about me.

"We need to give her time."

"I think it would be good for her to get out of this house."

What? Now, I'm moving?

"So soon?"

"Claire, think about it. If she had gone away to school, she would have already graduated and would probably be living on her own right now."

I know he's right, but I am about to have a panic attack from just thinking about leaving now.

"What if I'm not ready for her to go?"

I don't need to see her right now to know she's crying. My father is comforting her now.

I only hear, "Shh…shh."

I feel guilty for eavesdropping, and I hurry to make a plate of leftover fruit and cheese for breakfast. I take it outside to join them.

My mom waves my dad away and tries to act like she wasn't just crying. He gently squeezes my arm as I walk past before he walks farther out into the backyard and inspects one of his birdhouses.

"You slept in." She remarks.

I nod. "Yesterday was…"

She puts her elbows on the table and places her chin on top of her hands. Her hair is long enough that she has it pulled back in a ponytail. A breeze makes my hair swirl around my head and sometimes into my mouth as I try to eat.

"I know, sweetie."

"How are you doing?"

She gives me a tight smile, lowering one of her hands to pat my forearm. It's then that she notices I'm wearing Ally's cardigan. Her fingertips ghost over the weave. She pulls her hand back and wipes her eyes before standing. Then, she wipes her hands on her pants.

I hesitate, before asking, "Is it okay?"

Her tight smile is now more a grimace. She nods quickly, leaving her plate on the table, and she hurries inside. I glance over at my dad to see he was watching us.

"Everything okay?" he asks, walking back over.

I roll my lips between my teeth, pushing them together.

"Aubrey?"

"I'm wearing Ally's sweater, Dad."

His shoulders sag. He pulls off his glasses and rubs his eyes. "I'm going—"

"It's okay, Dad." I know he's going to go check on her.

We have spent the last six years with a common goal—helping Ally get better. Now that she's gone, I'm not sure any of us know what to do.

Do I go back to school? I'm not sure if I want to go back. So much feels pointless now. What hurts the most is the person who always gave me the best advice is gone.

When I overheard my mom say she isn't ready for me to leave, I felt my own agreement. I'm not ready to leave either.

There isn't a way to reclaim my college experience. I don't see myself being a senior living in a dorm. I also cannot picture myself in an off-campus apartment either.

I look down at my plate. The slices of cheese have warmed. I wrinkle my nose. Unless it's queso or fondue, I do not like warm cheese. I push away from the table. I'm done eating, but I'm not ready to go inside yet. I walk out into the middle of the yard and sink down, Indian-style.

After a moment, I lie back in the grass, closing my eyes. When I feel a shadow pass over me, I blink my eyes open. A large cloud has moved in front of the sun. The cloud is more gray than white. Its bottom is an even darker gray. I wonder if it will rain. The idea is a pleasant one. A sprinkle, not a downpour. It makes me think of an expression or saying I've heard. Something about rain at a memorial or funeral means God is crying. It sounds romantic—the concept that God would share in our grief.

I know it's bullshit though because there wasn't a cloud in the sky during Ally's memorial. People say things that aren't true to make themselves feel better. It's a lie though, and all it does is make people desperate to latch on to something in a time like this.

So, before I dismiss the idea as being stupid, I waste the time, thinking, *Wow, it didn't rain. That must mean God doesn't care about Ally.*

That is even worse for me since I'm not even sure I believe in God. These expressions mean nothing. They serve no purpose. Rain is rain, no matter when it falls. When the cloud passes, I stand and make my way back inside, collecting my plate on the way.

After putting it in the dishwasher, I take a lap around the first floor. No sign of Mom or Dad. Knowing that wearing Ally's cardigan sent my mother back to bed crushes me. I take it off, rolling it into a ball in my hands, and I walk upstairs.

Once I'm in my room, I put it in the back of my closet, covering it with an old sleeping bag. It bothers me that a sweater that gives me comfort can cause my mom pain. I want to feel closer to Ally, but hurting my mom is the last thing I want to do.

Ally would have known what to do. She had this way of knowing exactly what to say in any situation. I only seem to make things worse, no matter how hard I try.

I don't want to be sad all the time. That isn't going to change anything. That won't bring her back. I just don't know what to do otherwise. Deciding that talking to my dad might be a good start, I take a shower and pull on some sweats before heading back downstairs.

My dad is in the kitchen, condensing the leftovers from the memorial into fewer containers. I stand next to him and start stacking the empty trays, so they'll take up less space in the recycling bin.

"How's Mom?" I ask once I'm out of trays.

He takes a deep breath. "She's doing the best she can. It'll just take her some time."

"I feel like I'm making it worse for her."

He reaches out to tuck a strand of hair behind my ear. "I think you remind her of her."

I nod. It makes sense. Ally and I always looked like we could be sisters. Same height, build, same auburn hair, and hazel eyes. My mom must have seen her ghost every time she looked at me. I quickly brush away a tear, not wanting him to see me cry.

"I just don't know what to do, Dad."

"In what way, sweetie?"

"I feel like I need to be doing something. I just don't know what. I missed fall enrollment, but I'm not even sure I want to go back to school. I just don't know what to do."

He pulls one of the kitchen chairs out and sits, putting his elbow on the table and resting his chin on it. "I wonder if it was a mistake, letting you stay here instead of going to Yale."

I start to interrupt him, but he shakes his hand to stop me.

"It's just that you probably would have been done with school and living on your own by now."

My jaw drops. "Do you not want me living here?"

He shakes his head. "No, sweetie. I just feel like we robbed you of your independence. That the only reason you're so unsure of what you want is because we held you back."

"There's no way I would have gone away to school even if you guys wanted me to."

He shrugs.

I get what he's saying though. How can I know what I want out of life if I haven't lived?

My senior year of high school, I thought I had it all. I had a boyfriend. I was going to Yale. It's six years later. I have an associate's degree in computer science. I haven't dated. I still live at home.

Mike, the guy I dated in high school, is married now. I think his wife is even already expecting. Stuff like that makes me stay away from Facebook.

I feel like I don't fit in with the people who used to be my friends. They're either partying or settling down. There doesn't seem to be an in-between, and right now, I don't fit into either category.

FOUR

Mr. Clark, the attorney handling Ally's estate, is here to read her will.

I talked to my dad about it earlier. He thinks it's just a formality. Ally didn't have any tangible assets toward the end.

We're all in the living room, my mom and dad on the sofa. I sit in one of the armchairs while Mr. Clark stands by my dad's desk.

He clears his throat to get our attention. "I'm here today to read the will of Allison Chanthom. She asked that Drew, Claire, and Aubrey Kline be here for the reading." He glances at each of us as he says our names.

"Ms. Chanthom requests that all her earthly possessions go to her elder sister, Claire, and Claire's husband, Drew."

My dad starts to stand to thank him for coming out. Mr. Clark holds up his finger to stop him.

He lifts another piece of paper off the desk and continues to read, "To her niece, Aubrey Kline, Ms. Chanthom leaves the proceeds of this life insurance policy. The policy is valued at fifty thousand dollars."

My mouth drops. She did what?

He sets the page back down and pauses. "It is her intention that these assets be utilized to fund a trip for Ms. Kline to go to the locations on her When I Get Better board."

I sit there, shell-shocked, as my mom and dad both stand to read the will themselves. I half listen as Mr. Clark presents a letter my aunt wrote to my mom and my dad. My dad reads it out loud to my mom.

"She wants Aubrey to go by herself?" my mom asks.

"She just doesn't want either of us to go with her." My dad glances over at me.

"Why?" My mom pulls the letter closer, so she can see.

"Something about gaining independence."

Mr. Clark is behind them, collecting his things. He leaves some forms for my parents and me before excusing himself.

I don't envy his job, I think as I hear him close the front door.

I'm still trying to process the news—a trip, her trip. Ally wants me to take her trip. I've never been out of the country, let alone around the world.

I look at my parents. Their heads are together as they read and reread her letter. I picture the Better board, still upstairs in her room. I don't

need to see it to remember the pictures on it.
They're etched into my memory.

I ask to see her letter when it looks as though
my parents are done with it. My dad looks at my
mom, waiting for her to nod her head, before he
gives it to me. It's handwritten on simple white
paper. There are no lines, and I'm struck by how
level each row is. I wonder when she wrote it, and
I flip it over to look for a date before I start
reading. She wrote it only six months ago, while
we were trying to get her approved for that clinical
trial.

"Do they sell life insurance to people with
cancer?" I ask.

My dad flips through the pages Mr. Clark left
on his desk before he finds the life insurance policy.
"It's under a group plan through her work. She
must have bought it before she knew."

I nod, looking back down at the letter. It's
weird, reading a letter written to someone else.

> *Dearest Claire and Drew,*
>
> *If you are reading this letter, it means I
> am gone. I want to thank you for taking
> such good care of me. I am so lucky to
> have you both and Aubrey in my life.
> There are many times your love alone
> kept me going.*

I know what you all gave up to take care of me as well. I don't have much to repay you all with. My love—please know you have my love.

I want to try to do something for Aubrey. I have a small life insurance policy that I have named her the beneficiary of. I want her to go on my trip, the one I was supposed to take when I got better.

There is no legal obligation. (I checked with Mr. Clark.) It is only my last wish that she do this.

We all know how much Aubrey gave up when she stayed back to help with me. I know you both still see her as your little girl, but she's a woman now. She needs to gain some independence away from the two of you. She needs an opportunity to grow and learn to trust herself and her choices.

While there is nothing making her take this trip, I have one request if she does. Neither of you—I repeat, neither of you—are to go with her. Give her a chance to find herself apart from you.

*Without this, I fear she will end up
living with you two forever, and I will
blame myself and be forced to come back
to show my displeasure. I have no desire
to come back and haunt any of you. I
will be much too busy flirting with James
Dean.*

*Please let her do this. Let her have an
adventure.*

*I love you both bigger than the whole
wide world.*

Ally

As I lower her letter, I feel their eyes on me.
They expect a reaction, but I have nothing to give
them. I don't know how I feel about it.

I'm not sure I want to go. I'm scared of going.
And by myself? It's a crazy idea. I wouldn't know
what to do. I've been on a plane but never by
myself. It is exciting though—the idea of seeing the
world. I'm not sure which consumes me more, the
fear or the excitement.

Besides, her letter only *asks* them to let me go
alone. There is no guarantee either of them will let
me go alone.

My dad clears his throat, "Well?"

I look up at my dad. "I can't go around the
world."

"See." He looks at my mom and gestures toward me.

"Drew"—she puts her hand on his forearm—"it's what Ally wanted."

He walks back over to the sofa. "But—"

"We'll figure it out," she interrupts. Then, she turns to me. "I think you should do this."

My eyes widen. "Mom…"

I've spent most of the afternoon in my room, looking at Ally's Better board. My parents are downstairs, discussing Ally's letter. My dad thinks the idea is crazy, if not foolish. My mom only wants to fulfill Ally's wishes. Only yesterday, I heard my mom say she wasn't ready for me to leave, but now, she's pushing me to.

I'm sitting on the floor in front of my bed with my legs crossed. The Better board is propped up in front of me. There are six pictures on it—the Sydney Opera House, Victoria Falls, Cristo Redentor, the Eiffel Tower, the Great Wall of China, and lastly, a beach in the Caribbean.

When she picked these pictures, she didn't mean that she wanted to go to each specific place, but she wanted to travel to each region. One picture for six of the seven continents. She had no desire to visit Antarctica.

I tilt my head, trying to picture myself in each shot. I squint. I close one eye. No matter what I try, I can't see it. I'm not a girl who can travel around the world. I won't go. They can't make me. I cringe, thinking of Ally. The idea of not doing something she wanted is impossible. No matter what, I have to do this—for her.

I go downstairs, walk up to my parents, and interrupt them. "Mom, Dad, stop."

They both look over at me.

"I want to do this. It's what Ally wanted. Does the idea of going to another country all by myself scare me? Yes, a lot, but she wouldn't have asked me to do this if she hadn't thought I could."

"I don't like it," my dad mumbles.

"Dad."

He takes off his glasses and rubs his hand over his face. "Okay, I know she asked that your mom and I not go, but how about you travel with a companion?"

"I don't need a babysitter," I groan.

"That's not what I'm saying. There are tours and travel guides. It might make me feel better if you were part of a group."

I look at my mom. She smiles, trying to reassure me.

"I guess that would be okay." I relent.

I walk over to sit next to my mom on the sofa while my dad starts talking about my getting a passport and traveler's checks.

45

My mind is racing. When will I go? Where will I go? Can I actually even do this? Alone?

When I was ten, I spent the summer with my dad's parents in New Hampshire. I'd traveled by myself. My mom had stayed with me at the gate until I boarded the plane. It had been a direct flight to Manchester. My grandma had been waiting for me at the gate there. The experience was equally terrifying and exhilarating.

It wasn't the first time I had flown, but it was the first time I had flown by myself. My whole flight, I remembered being so afraid my grandma wouldn't be there for me. I don't know why I was so scared. I didn't have a reason to doubt she would be there.

My family was nothing if not punctual. Any lesson or practice I had growing up, soccer or dance, my mom or dad was on time to pick me up. Not once were they late.

My fear of my grandma not being there was irrational. I can see that now.

This trip will be different. There won't be someone waiting for me, to hold my hand at each stop. I don't want to admit it, but maybe having a travel companion is a good idea.

I'm just not sure if that's what Ally wanted for me or not. If she wanted me to do this by myself, I want to respect that. However, I don't see her wanting me to be scared or alone in a foreign place either. She thought this would be good for me, and I trust her.

Paperwork, my existence has become one form after another. There are forms to open an account in my name to deposit Ally's life insurance into. There's a passport application. There are temporary visas to apply for. All of this takes time, and I have to write my name, date of birth, social security number, and address over and over again.

It will hopefully take three weeks to get my passport. I need a visa for Australia, China, and Zambia but not for Peru or France.

Plus, I'm not sure those are the places I want to go to. Do I want to see the Great Wall of China or the hustle and bustle of Tokyo? Do I want to see the Great Barrier Reef or the Outback? Machu Picchu or Rio? I'm not sure.

Where I will go and how long I will be at each place has so many variables to consider. Local climate and the differences in seasons south of the equator is a factor as well.

My mom and I pour over travel guides and handbooks. Planning this trip is giving her a reason to get out of bed every day. She wants to know I will be as prepared as possible.

My dad, when he isn't working, researches different sightseeing tour groups. If he had it his way, I'd do the whole trip cruise-style. One dedicated bed the whole time with stops to various ports along the way. I'm not opposed to taking a cruise at some point on my trip, especially in the Caribbean, but I don't want to do that the whole time.

In one of the travel books, my mom and I are reading about France. It talks about scouts and how they will backpack all over in small groups. I want to try that—backpacking. I don't know if I'd like it, but from the pictures, it looks like it could be fun. How will I ever find out what I like if I don't try different things?

My dad isn't thrilled with this argument. I love him. I know he just wants to keep me safe. I wish he would relax a bit though. His anxiety is starting to wear on me. My mom is the opposite. She is full speed ahead, ready for me to go and figure it out on my own. I need them to meet somewhere in the middle and figure out a safe way for me to experience things.

"You two are driving me crazy."

Their heads snap up to look at me.

"What?" My dad lifts a brow at me.

"This trip. You two." I wave my finger back and forth between them.

My mom folds her arms across her chest and leans back into the sofa. "Care to elaborate, Aubrey?"

Why did I open my mouth? "All right, Dad is going overboard on the safety precautions, and you don't seem to be worried at all. I would love some balance."

One corner of my dad's mouth pulls up into a half grin. "So, I need to relax, and your mom needs to act more stressed. Is that right?"

"Dad," I groan. Then, I think about it. "Well, when you put it like that, yeah."

My mom rolls her eyes. "I'm just trying to be supportive."

"Thank you. I appreciate it, but stop pointing out hang gliding and bungee jumping, please. Not going to happen."

My dad glares at her. "Bungee jumping?"

She shrugs. "Ally always wanted to try it."

I look down. "I never knew that."

She gets a faraway look in her eyes. "Ally wanted it all. I used to think her dreams were crazy. She joked about going over Niagara Falls in a barrel, swimming with sharks, climbing Mt. Everest. She was fearless when she was little. She must have given me a hundred heart attacks."

"What did she do?" I ask, leaning forward.

She shakes her head, laughing. "One time, she staged a girls-against-boys war in the neighborhood we grew up in. I was doing homework on our back deck. She and a bunch of kids were in the woods behind our house. She appointed herself lookout and climbed to the top of a small pine tree. She was screaming at the top of her lungs that the boys were coming, and she must have moved around too much. The top of the tree broke off, and she fell with it. She had to have hit every branch on the way down."

She paused to lick her lips. "I run over to check on her. The first thing out of her mouth was, 'The boys are coming.' I could have strangled her."

"Was she hurt?"

My mom flicked her hand at the wrist. "She had a bump on the back of her head. She refused to let me put ice on it. She was so stubborn." Her fingertips brush moisture away from the corners of her eyes.

"Mom, don't cry."

"It's okay, sweetie. It feels nice to talk about her."

"I remember she didn't think I was good enough for you." My dad smiles.

"She was right. You're not." She laughs.

"Mom!"

"Settle down, honey. I'm joking."

My dad stands and comes over to sit next to my mom on the couch. He pulls her toward him and loudly kisses her cheek.

I look at them. His arms are wrapped around her waist. My mom is blushing, and they're both smiling. It's nice to see them look happy. As much as they both grieve Ally, it's good that they still have each other.

Other than my parents, who do I have?

FIVE

I slept in again. I can hear my dad on the phone. He sounds excited about something.

I wave as I walk past the living room on my way to the kitchen. My mom is at the table, flipping through a travel magazine.

"Hey, who's Dad on the phone with?" I ask, making myself a bowl of cereal.

Her brows come together as she thinks about it. "A coworker, I think. Don something or other."

"Oh." Since I don't know who he is, I don't really care anymore.

"Look at this hotel, sweetie." My mom pats the seat of the chair next to her.

I set my bowl down before sliding in. I make encouraging noises as I eat, so she continues to point out different pictures from the magazine. I am nodding at the well-appointed attached bath of an Australian hotel when my dad walks in.

My mom and I both look up at him. He's grinning. I haven't seen him this happy in…I'm not sure how long.

He rubs his hands together. "Guess what?"

Okay, I think I'll bite. "What?"

"I just got you a travel guide for the whole trip."

"Huh?" I say while my mom says, "What do you mean?"

My mom and I look at each other before looking back at my dad, who still looks thrilled.

"Remember Don Burke?"

My mom nods.

"His son, Adam, is a photographer."

We stare at him.

He rolls his eyes and gestures with his hands. "A travel photographer."

My mouth drops. "You want me to travel around the world with some guy I've never met?"

His smile drops a fraction. "He's already been to some of the places you want to go to. He knows how to travel overseas." He looks at his hands and then back up at me. "I thought you'd be happy."

Now, I've hurt his feelings. "Well, how old is he?"

"Under thirty, maybe twenty-eight. I know you don't know him, but it would make me feel so much better about this"—he gestures to the travel magazines on the table—"trip if you went with someone."

"But what if I don't like him?" I cringe at how whiny I sound.

"I'm sure he's a nice boy." My mom pats my arm. "I also like the idea of having someone with you."

"How did this happen? The last thing we talked about was the group tours, picking up a new one at each city."

My dad takes off his glasses, setting them on the table, before he rubs his eyes. "I didn't expect you to be upset."

He didn't answer my question. I lift my brows.

"I had a conference call last week. The line was open, and we were just talking while we waited for more people to log on. Beth asked how the trip plans were going. Don was on the call, and he mentioned Adam was planning a trip. The call got started, but afterward, I rang Don to find out where Adam was planning on going. He gave me Adam's number, and I called him. I wanted to know where he was headed to see if any of your locations would overlap. He was only planning to visit South America."

"Then, how is he able to go for the whole trip?"

His eyes flick to my mom's. "I, uh…offered to sponsor the rest."

"You didn't." I shake my head.

"I thought you'd be happy about this." He looks miserable.

I stand, and the legs of my chair protest loudly. "What if we don't get along? Will I be stuck with him the whole time?"

"Aubrey…"

"Dad…" I mimic his tone.

"Please, honey, think about it."

"But—"

"Sweetie…"

Great. Now, my mom is in on it.

"I don't need a babysitter."

"He won't be a babysitter, Aubrey. He's only a few years older than you."

"Can I think about it? Or is it already decided?"

He hesitates.

"Dad! So, I have no say in this?"

He shakes his head. "I didn't say anything, Aubrey." He gestures toward my chair. "Why don't you sit back down?"

"Don't want to."

"I'm not going to say that Adam has to go, but I wouldn't know what to tell Don. Will you at least think about it?"

I roll my eyes. "Ally wanted me to be independent. I don't like the idea of having someone with me the whole time. I know you said he wouldn't be a babysitter, but that's what it would feel like to me."

I take a deep breath and try to gauge their expressions. They both look crushed.

"Ugh, fine. I'll think about it," I mumble as I walk out.

I have zero intentions of actually going along with it. This is my trip. I'm doing this for Ally. She wanted me to do this by myself. If I'm supposed to be gaining my independence, the last thing I need is a babysitter. I just need to figure out a way to convince my parents that I'll be fine.

Worst case, maybe I can talk this Adam guy into going somewhere else—without me. I fight the urge to slam my bedroom door, trying to drive home how mature I am. Maybe reverse psychology will work. I could act like I think it's a great idea, and my dad might change his mind.

Don't they realize the money is in an account in my name? The only thing stopping me from leaving tomorrow is the fact that I don't have my visas or passport yet. That, and the fact that I don't know what I'm doing. It's just that having someone, a stranger who I might not like, with me the entire time sucks.

I'm twenty-four, and I still live at home with my parents. Sure, some kids my age move back in with their parents after college. Me? I never moved out.

I sag onto my bed, tucking my legs under me. I need this. I need to get out of this house and be by myself for a while. I'm tired of walking past Ally's door every day and her not being there. Sometimes, I still forget, and I go to open her door. Then, I remember. I stand there with my hand on the knob, reality hitting me that she's gone.

Maybe the reason I'm so against this Adam guy going is because the only person I would have ever wanted to go with is gone. Adam, whoever he is, makes a sucky replacement.

I don't always cry these days when I think about Ally. Sometimes, I can think about good times and smile or even laugh but not today. Today, the hole in my world created by her absence feels too fresh. She would have known what to say to make it better. She always did. No matter how wrong I was, she'd take my side and make my parents see as well.

I need her so bad. I'd be okay if she could just hug me or talk to me for a single minute. Days like today make me feel like I will never be okay again, like I will always feel like a part of me is missing.

Reaching for a tissue, I grab the box and peer inside it to see that it's empty. I head to the bathroom and grab a roll of toilet paper. I blow my nose loudly as I stand in front of the sink.

My mom is standing outside the door when I walk out. Her face crumples when she sees my tears. Guilt blows through me. I try so hard to keep this from her. I don't want my grief to trigger hers. I want to be strong and there for her.

"I didn't know," she croaks.

"It's okay, Mom. I know."

I lean against her, allowing her arms to envelop me. I lift my head to see my dad trudging up the stairs.

His eyes widen when he sees us. He walks over and asks, "What's wrong?"

I answer the simplest way I know how. "I miss her."

My mom rubs my back. "I do too, sweetie. I do too."

Seeing them, their concern, it finally hits me. They just want me to be safe. I don't want to argue anymore right now. It doesn't feel right. Now is about missing Ally.

"I'm just going to go lie down."

I pull back, and my mom's arms hover before she lets them fall to her sides. My dad tucks her under his arm, and she leans into him. They're still standing like that, just outside the hall bathroom, when I close my door.

I set the roll of toilet paper on my bedside table and lie down. My room feels too bright, so I stand back up to adjust the blinds. Once I'm on my bed again, I start my one-sided conversation. This has become a form of comfort for me.

"I wish you were here," I whisper, closing my eyes.

I've read all these books about how someone dies, but the people who loved that person will somehow sense their presence I will myself to sense her. Something, her perfume, her warmth, anything.

I want a picture to fall off the wall or a sudden thunderstorm to pop up. If I love her, I should still be able to feel her. It feels wrong that I don't. If she's a ghost, does that mean she's moved on? It still doesn't feel right that she's gone. It's like some cosmic joke. She has to be just waiting in the wings, and then she'll jump out and say, *Gotcha*, at the right moment.

I am prepared to believe in any possibility that doesn't involve her just being gone. I stare up at the ceiling. My fan is on its lowest setting, doing lazy circles above my head. I watch the blades go around and around.

"Why don't you talk to him?" My dad shrugs.

"I can't call some guy I don't know," I argue.

"It's the only way you'll have a chance to talk before you meet."

My forehead wrinkles. "What do you mean, the only chance?"

He smirks at me. He always does this when he has to repeat something to me. "Don't you remember? He lives in New York."

"In the city?"

"I think so."

My mom sets down her fork and picks up her napkin to wipe her mouth. "How exciting."

I push my dinner around on my plate. After my dad catches my eye, I take another bite.

"We wouldn't even meet before the trip?" I ask.

"He has limited funds. I thought if you go to Europe first, you could fly out together from New York."

I tilt my head. "You are seriously fine with me traveling around the world with someone you've never even met?"

He takes off his glasses and pinches the bridge of his nose. He inhales and exhales a few times before he puts his glasses back on and looks at me. "I am not thrilled with the idea of you being out there, alone. Don is a good man, and his son sounds like one as well. It's not ideal, but it's better than knowing you'll be in the care of complete strangers in every country you go to."

I hate to admit it, but I can see his logic. "Fine," I grumble. "As long as he doesn't boss me around. And what happens if we don't get along?"

My mom starts to say something but stops. My dad reaches out to hold her hand across the table.

"This trip is about growing up. Sometimes, in life, you will be forced to deal with people you dislike. Part of being a mature, independent grown-up is learning to be diplomatic."

As long as I live at home, I know he'll never see me as anything other than his little girl. As excited as I am about exploring new places, I also plan to figure out what I'm going to do once it's over. I know my parents won't like the idea, but once I'm back, I plan to move out. This trip will give me time to decide in what direction I plan to go.

Right now, I'm not sure whether I should go back to school or try to get a job. Nothing glamorous. Maybe I could waitress or be a nanny.

When I was in high school, I thought I wanted to be a doctor. I've heard stories about people who go on to medical school after being sick themselves or taking care of a sick loved one. Watching Ally had the opposite effect on me. I want nothing to do with anything remotely related to the medical field

After six years of part-time community college, I still don't have my degree. If I go back to school, I'll have to pick a major, which is kind of hard to do since I'm not sure what direction I want to go in.

I realize my parents are waiting for me to respond. "So, when should I call him?"

My dad's face breaks out into a wide grin. "Tomorrow should be good. It's probably too late tonight with the time difference."

After dinner, I hang back in the kitchen to rinse our plates and load the dishwasher. My parents go into the living room. Once I'm finished, I go to join them. I pause just outside the doorway when I hear them talking. I lean against the wall and listen.

"I'm worried about her," my mom says quietly.

"Aubrey will be fine. It's you I'm worried about. Have you thought about it?"

I hear her sigh.

"Do you really think it's necessary?"

"I do."

I wonder what they're talking about. I lean closer to the doorway and cringe when the floorboards beneath me let out a loud creak. Knowing they had to have heard that, I walk into the room and sit down, trying my best to look innocent.

They drop whatever they were talking about once I'm in the room. They talk about my dad's job while I flip through a travel magazine. Ever since Ally's letter was read, our house has been buried in them. Most of them come out only once a month. How my mom has acquired so many, I'll never know. I read an article about extreme travelers who hike and camp.

Cringing, I look over at my mom and dad. "This Adam guy won't want to camp, will he? I was hoping to stay in hotels."

My dad gives me a funny look before laughing. "You won't have to camp, honey."

I'm not sure why my question is so funny. Is he implying that I can't camp? I can camp, I think. I even briefly considered backpacking on this trip until I remembered I prefer air conditioning, soft mattresses, and hot showers to the great outdoors.

It's just good to know the plan of staying in hotels isn't changing now that this guy will be with me.

I go back to the article I was reading. There are so many things to consider when traveling overseas. Laundry is one of them. I keep seeing ads for quick-dry underwear that you hand-wash versus finding a Laundromat. It might be a good idea to purchase some. I'll just wait until my dad is not around to talk about it.

I need to figure out what clothes to pack that will be good for the whole trip. Depending on weather, we will spend the first part of our travels north of the equator, and we will move south just in time for the summer down there.

I read until the words start to get blurry, and then I head to bed. After I've brushed my teeth and washed my face, I'm not as tired as I was downstairs.

I turn on my laptop, so I can Google Adam. His name is fairly common. It's a mistake to click on images. There's a comedian, a few guys in the military, and a bunch of mug shots.

I hope that he isn't any of those before I add photographer to the search field. A Twitter handle pops up. I don't personally tweet, but the link takes me to a profile page that I think might be his. His profile picture is not a close-up, and it's him holding a camera in front of his face. Clever.

I shut down my laptop. I figure I can try to Internet-stalk him another day.

SIX

Why am I so nervous?

I hear the ringing in my ear as I look over at my dad. He's sitting at his desk. My mom is sitting on the sofa next to me.

"Hello?"

I gulp. "Hi. May I please speak with Adam Burke?"

"I'm Adam."

I pause.

He says, "Hello?"

"I'm Aubrey Kline. My dad thought it'd be a good idea for us to talk." I cringe as I say each word, not understanding why I feel so awkward.

"Okay."

He sounds bored, and now that I'm actually on the phone with him, I have no idea what to say. I roll the side of my bottom lip between my teeth and rub my tongue back and forth across it as I shrug at my parents.

After a long, uncomfortable pause, he says, "Is there anything you wanted to talk about, Aubrey?"

"Um…" It's like my brain is empty—well, not entirely empty. I suddenly have a Lady Gaga song that I don't like stuck in my head. I can't talk about that.

I panic and hand the phone to my mom before dropping my head in my hands. What is wrong with me?

"Hi, Adam," she says brightly. "This is Claire Kline, Aubrey's mom. She, um…had to run."

I close my eyes. I had to run? Run where? Not a great way to show my parents how mature I am. I don't even want to think about what Adam is thinking of this call. I tilt my head to look at my mom. She doesn't talk long, and she sets the phone in her lap when she's done.

"What was that about, Aubrey?"

"I don't know. I got nervous and froze," I groan.

She rubs my back. "He seemed like a nice young man. You have no reason to be nervous, hon."

We both look over at my dad, who is trying hard not to laugh.

"Not cool, Dad," I grumble.

My mom and dad just look at each other before they both start laughing.

"It wasn't that funny." I cross my arms over my chest and sink back into the couch.

"I'm not laughing," my mom argues despite that she is in fact laughing.

"Right." I glare at her. "If I'm socially awkward, I only have you two to blame, so keep on laughing."

"I'm sorry, sweetie." My dad coughs and swallows any lingering laughs.

"Why do you think you froze?" My mom leans her shoulder against mine.

I shake my head and look up at the ceiling. "I wanted to make a good impression, and then I just got nervous and couldn't think of anything to say. He has to think I'm mental."

"Maybe he just thinks you were busy."

I give her a look. "Busy enough to call him and then not talk? Yeah, that makes sense."

"Or," my dad interrupts, "he will think what I have known for some time. Women are crazy."

"Drew," My mom exclaims.

"Tell me I'm wrong." He smirks.

My mom and I look at each other and shrug. It's hard to argue.

"Not like you're sane." She huffs.

He stands and walks over to kiss her forehead. "Never said I was."

I get up and head toward the kitchen, preferring not to be around them when they're acting mushy. I grab an apple and go out to the backyard to eat it.

My travel papers arrived in the mail yesterday.

My dad has been emailing back and forth with Adam about booking flights and hotels. I'll be flying to New York in two days. I'm staying that night at Adam's apartment. Then, we're flying out to London the next morning.

My bags are basically packed. I have one giant rolling suitcase and a solar backpack. My mom has gone a bit overboard with catalog shopping. I have quick-dry underwear, a handheld water purifier, a plug adapter, a baggage scale, and any other random gadget that will supposedly make traveling easier.

My dad also upgraded my cell phone to an international plan and loaded a bunch of travel apps on it.

There's only one thing I care about in my luggage—a small wooden box with Celtic carvings on the sides. A smaller plastic container fits inside it. Inside that container are Ally's ashes. This will always be her trip, and I need her with me.

My mom cried when I asked if I could have some of her ashes. My dad, ever the planner, logged on to our airline's website to make sure it was legal to fly with them. Once he was able to confirm it was, my mom ordered the box to hold them.

For me, the only thing that matters on this trip is that Ally makes it to the places she dreamed of.

Now that most of the trip plans are done, my mom and dad have more time to themselves. My dad is cutting back his hours at work. Before Ally got sick, he was looking forward to retiring. Full retirement is on hold for now because their finances took a hit from taking care of Ally. Part of me feels guilty for spending money on this trip, but my parents refused to take any of Ally's insurance money.

My mom is volunteering at a local animal shelter. My dad gets nervous every time she mentions bringing a puppy home. It's only a matter of time before she does it.

I spend most of my time on the computer. For practice, I've printed out common phrases for every country we're traveling to. I also keep checking the hotel websites and looking at pictures of the suites.

My dad didn't like the idea of Adam and me sharing a room, but he didn't want me to be alone either. He settled on booking us suites or rooms with a connecting doorway for most of the trip. We won't get any of the room numbers until we check in, so I won't know what kind of views we'll have until we get there.

We aren't staying at hotels the whole time. Adam has friends that we'll stay with in London, and we're staying with an old friend of my mom's in Brazil.

I'm excited and nervous at the same time. I can't wait for my trip to start, but I'm afraid of the unknown. Traveling can be dangerous. My mom wouldn't have bought me a secret wallet I can wrap around my ankle if it weren't.

I've become shy and nervous over the last few years. I wasn't like this in high school. I wasn't crazy popular, but I had lots of friends and a boyfriend.

Ally's illness changed me. I know I will never be the person I was before, but I don't want to be who I am now either. I want to be brave. If my parents found out what I'm planning, they would probably cancel the trip. That's why I'm careful to delete my browsing history every night.

My mom pops her head in my doorway. "Still want to come with?"

I look up and nod. I stand and grab my purse to follow her. I'm tagging along with her to the animal shelter today and tomorrow. I figure I'll be doing a lot of walking during my travels, and I can practice with all of dogs that need to be walked at the shelter. This isn't the first time I've gone with her. Being around the animals relaxes me.

When we get there, she heads straight to the back office while I make my way to the kennels.

"Hey, George," I call out to another volunteer. "Who needs walking?"

He passes me a leash. "Trixie and Morton are the only ones who have been on a long walk since I've been here."

It's still early. "I'll start with Herman." I gesture toward a German shepherd mix. "Hi, Herman. Who's a good boy? You are. Yes, you are," I coo as I open his kennel.

He jumps on me, trying to lick my face. I clip the leash to his collar, and then while his front paws are still on me, I scratch his sides. He leans into the scratch, throwing his head back. I laugh and push him down. I wave to George as Herman and I make our way behind the shelter. I grab a waste bag on the way and shove it into my pocket.

There's a field before a wooded area with walking trails behind the shelter. Sometimes, I'll play Frisbee with the well-behaved dogs in the field.

I learned the hard way that Herman is not trustworthy off the leash. I spent one afternoon chasing him through the woods. I won't make that mistake again. He's full of energy this morning, and he does more bouncing than walking.

I tried to talk my mom into adopting him, but if she convinces my dad to get a dog, she wants a small one.

It's cool in the shade. Other than the occasional squirrel, Herman and I match each other's pace easily.

I take the longer trail, talking to Herman as we walk. "Are you going to miss me, buddy?"

He just looks at me, tongue hanging out. I take that as a yes.

"I'm going to miss you too. Before I leave tomorrow, I promise I'll remind George that you like the long trail."

He isn't paying attention. Instead, he is fully focused on smelling the post of a sign. I have to tug him to get him to start walking again.

After our walk, I let him jump on me and lick me before putting him back in his kennel.

"Is he a good dog?"

I turn and see a woman in the doorway. She's curiously looking at Herman.

I gulp. "He's a great dog, just active. He loves to walk."

I reach my fingertips into his kennel, letting him lick them. Inside my head, I hope she won't adopt him. I plaster a smile on my face, and I let her know that we have a room where she can hang out with any of the dogs she might be interested in. I gesture toward George, letting her know that he can help her.

I hook the leash to a beagle and go back outside. Sampson, the beagle, is an older dog. Instead of heading into the woods, we make a wide lap around the field. He's panting and goes straight for his water dish when we come back inside.

Herman isn't in his kennel. I sigh and take out the next dog. All the while, I hope that Herman will be back in his kennel when I get back. He still isn't there though when I do come back.

George sees me staring at his kennel. "Hey, that lady adopted him."

I nod. I figured as much. I force a half smile before I head out with another dog. When I get back, I get some water and hang out with my mom in the back office, so I can sit in front of a fan for a while.

"I heard Herman got adopted."

I nod. "The lady seemed nice. I hope she takes good care of him."

Once my mom is done, we head home, and on the way, we grab some takeout for lunch. My dad is napping in the hammock in the backyard. My mom shakes his shoulder, awaking him.

"You're getting red."

He pulls her down next to him. She laughs as he kisses the side of her head. I'm happy for them. It will be good for them to have me out of their hair. I sit at the kitchen table and start eating. They walk in together a couple of minutes later.

I snort when I see my dad. "How long were you out there?"

He looks confused. "Not long." He looks at my mom. "Why?"

She looks away, covering her mouth with her hand.

"Dad, go look in the mirror."

We hear his groan when he sees himself. He looks like a semi-sunburned Two-Face from *Batman*. He walks back into the kitchen, giving us dirty looks as we giggle.

We don't talk while we eat. The silence is only disturbed by an occasional giggle. After lunch, my mom and dad go upstairs, so she can put cream on his face.

I sit in the backseat with my backpack next to me. As my dad drives to the airport, my mom looks back every few minutes, like she's checking to make sure I'm still there. Each time she looks back, I lift my eyebrows and grin at her. They're not sure I can do this. I'm not sure I can do this. I just can't let them know that.

I have a direct flight to JFK. Once my rolling case is checked, my mom and dad walk with me to the line for security.

"Call us once you've landed," my mom says, pulling me into a hug.

"I will," I murmur into her neck.

My dad pulls me into his arms next. "Have fun, sweetie. It's a once-in-a-lifetime experience. Just be safe."

I nod, not wanting to cry. I'm twenty-four. I should be able to say good-bye to my parents at an airport without tearing up.

As I weave my way through the rope maze, my parents stay and watch me. My dad's arm is casually slung around my mom's shoulders. She leans into him. When I get to the front of the line, I look back to blow them a kiss and give a final wave. They wave back, and I can tell my mom is crying. I square my shoulders and don't look back again. That way, they won't see that I'm crying.

Once I'm past security, I find a restroom, so I can wash my face. My flight will start boarding in forty-five minutes. I find an end seat at my gate and sink into it, tucking my backpack under my legs in front of me. I have a book, but I'm too nervous to read it. Instead, I people-watch.

There's a family of five—a mom, a dad, two boys, and a girl—in the seats facing mine. I envy the kids. I always wanted a brother or a sister when I was growing up. I guess that's why Ally filled that older sister void for me.

There's also a group of older women. It's not hard to figure out their plans. They have matching handmade T-shirts with puffy paint, letting everyone know they are Broadway bound. They're a loud group, laughing and joking with each other and anyone sitting near them. They lift my mood, and I can't help but smile at their antics.

As soon as I'm on the plane, that feeling is gone. I'm on my way to meet the stranger who I'm going to travel around the world with. A stranger who I have not even managed to have an actual conversation with. I know it shouldn't matter, but I'm worried about making a good first impression and what he's like. I have no interest in traveling with someone I can't get along with.

I have a direct flight, and I watch a movie on the way. Before I know it, we're descending. I have a window, and I am basically trapped until the people sitting next to me have gotten their things and are in the aisle.

Once I'm off the plane, I call my mom to let her know I've landed. She has bad news for me. Adam had something come up, and he will not be picking me up from the airport. She's going to text me his address, so I can take a cab to his apartment instead. He's going to leave a key with a neighbor for me. Awesome...or the opposite.

I make my way to baggage claim, and I have no trouble finding my giant suitcase. There's a queue for taxicabs right outside. I'm on my way to Adam's apartment in no time. As we flow through traffic, I feel a sense of pride bloom within me. I realize that even though I'm still in the States, I have managed to deal with a change in plans easily, and I am on my way to where I need to be by myself.

The cab pulls up in front of a six-story brick apartment building. I glance up and down the street. It's congested. I can't imagine trying to find a parking spot, but then I remember my mom said that Adam doesn't have a car. The cab driver pulls my suitcase from the trunk and leaves before I can thank him.

The main door to the building has a buzzer-type system to it. Adam's neighbor, Mr. Wiltshire, buzzes me in. I heft my suitcase up four flights of stairs. Mr. Wiltshire is there, waiting for me with the key. I thank him, and once I have Adam's door open, I practically fall into his apartment.

Once the door is locked behind me, I take a look around, mainly in search of a bathroom. The apartment is small, studio-style. I'm curious where I'm supposed to sleep tonight.

His style is minimalist. It makes sense, given how small the place is. I can't ignore the photos on his walls. The wall behind his sofa has exposed brick, and the photos are wire-mounted in brushed nickel frames. They're black-and-white photos of mountains, lakes, and lighthouses. There are also a series of objects—doorknobs, hinges, and rivets— in extreme close-up.

I linger at each one, captivated, until my stomach grumbles. I'm poking around his kitchen when he walks in with dinner in hand. I blush, closing the cabinet I was looking in, and I wave. My mouth drops when I see him. He really should update his avi because covering that face with a camera should be a crime.

He sets bags of takeout on the coffee table. "You must be Aubrey," he says, reaching out his hand.

I gulp when his hand folds around mine. He's tall with a lanky build and light brown hair that falls into his gray eyes. I repress the urge to reach up and run my fingers through his hair. My stomach clenches, an uncontrolled physical reaction to him.

I haven't had or even thought about sex in years. One glance at Adam at my body seemed to be waking from some sort of hibernation.

SEVEN

My hand is still in his. He seems to be appraising me. My free hand automatically moves to tuck a strand of hair behind my ear. I'm wearing jeans and a black T-shirt. I'm suddenly wishing I were wearing something cuter. He drops my hand, and I push it into my pocket.

"Italian good? I picked up some chicken alfredo on the way."

I cringe. I hate alfredo sauce, but I don't want to be rude. He didn't know.

"Maybe just a little bit." I sigh, and then I close my eyes and pray he did not just hear the dying whale sound my stomach just made.

I smell garlic and hope that means there are breadsticks. He reaches up, leaning into me, to open the cabinet behind me. I hold my breath as he pulls down two plates.

God, why did he have to get alfredo?

I follow him to the couch and watch as he spoons a ridiculous amount onto my plate.

Once both plates are ready, he looks up at me. "What do you want to drink? I have some beer or soda."

"Um…" I push the noodles around on my plate, trying not to gag. "Soda is good."

While he pours me a glass, I devour a breadstick. Part of me wants to ask if he has a strainer. I don't mind noodles, and if I can rinse the sauce off of them, I know I can eat it. I stab one noodle with my fork and attempt to wipe some of the sauce off by rubbing it against the plate before lifting it to my mouth. There is something about the smell that turns my stomach. Short of pinching my nose for each bite, I don't think I'll be able to eat any of it.

He's walking back over with my drink. I can't look him in the eye.

"I'm so sorry. I hate to do this, but do you have anything else I could eat?"

I cringe and look up at him. His hand is suspended, midair, reaching out to pass me my drink. He licks his bottom lip and leans down to set my drink next to me before straightening back up.

"Something wrong with the alfredo?" He tilts his head, waiting for my response.

"I just…I don't know why, but I'm a picky eater. There's something about the sauce. If you don't have anything else…" I think of his near empty cabinets. "If you have a strainer, I can still eat the noodles."

"I can go and get you something else." He sounds pissed.

"No, don't. I'm fine. I wasn't even that hungry."

He lifts a brow at me and smirks as my stomach chooses that moment to growl.

"I don't want to put you out. Please, if you have a strainer, I can still eat the noodles," I plead.

He reaches down, lifting my plate, and sets it on his kitchen counter. I want to disappear as I watch him strain my noodles.

He looks over his shoulder at me. "Do you want any kind of sauce?"

"Plain is good. Thank you."

He gives the noodles one final shake before dumping them back on my plate. He looks beyond annoyed when he sets the plate back in front of me.

"I'm sorry."

"It's fine," he mumbles while opening a beer.

I focus on eating the food in front of me. I'm starving. I can't believe I tried to tell him otherwise.

"So, is there a lot of stuff you don't eat? That could be an issue while traveling."

I gulp down the bite I'm working on. "I don't like seafood, and I just like plain stuff."

His jaw drops. "No seafood?"

I nod.

"No fish, shrimp, sushi, lobster? None?"

I hate these questions. I don't understand why it bothers people that I don't eat certain kinds of food. It's not like I have an issue with people eating stuff I don't like.

I reply with my canned response, "If it comes from the sea, it's not for me."

"You're missing out."

"That's a matter of opinion," I snap.

He shrugs, taking a long pull from his bottle. When I've finished, he takes my plate. I offer to wash it, but he shakes his head and does it himself. I want to ask what our sleeping arrangements will be, but I feel awkward bringing it up. I wonder if my dad would have booked me a hotel room if he had known Adam lived in a studio.

"Do you shower at night or in the morning?" he asks, walking back over.

I look over at him, confused. "Morning. Is that okay?"

"We have to get up early. I was going to shower tonight to save time."

"Oh, I can take a shower tonight. I just normally like to shower in the morning. It helps me wake up." I don't know why I told him that.

He turns and leans against the counter with his arms crossed in front of him. "What other things wake you up?" he teases.

I furrow my brow. "Caffeine, I guess."

He smirks. "I'm sure that can be arranged."

I clear my throat. "Not to change the subject, but where am I sleeping tonight?"

The sofa seems like the only logical answer, but there's only one, and if it's his bed…

I feel my cheeks redden just at the thought of sitting on what might be his bed.

One side of his mouth pulls up into a half smile. I don't like how looking at his mouth makes me feel. This trip is supposed to be about finding myself, not lusting after my babysitter.

"You're sleeping with me tonight."

Did he just say that?

"No, I'm not," I stammer.

He grins, pushing himself off the counter, and he walks toward me. I feel myself sinking into the sofa, trying to further the distance between us. When he gets to the coffee table, he pulls it to the side, closer to the door. There is nothing blocking him from me now. My mouth drops. He turns and opens double doors of what looks like an entertainment center. I exhale when I see it's a Murphy bed.

He grins at me. "Which do you want—sofa or bed?"

The idea of sleeping in his bed, laying my head on his pillow, surrounded by his scent excites me. I gulp. "Either is fine."

He nods. "Won't eat seafood but has no problem sleeping on a lumpy couch. Interesting."

I roll my eyes at the seafood dig.

"Can't even get you to try fish and chips while we're in England?"

I meet his eyes and smile sweetly. "Sure. Just hold the fish."

He closes the doors to the bed and sits back down next to me. He picks up his beer to take another swig. "Seriously, when was the last time you tried seafood?"

There seems to be two types of people in the world. There are people who, when told I don't eat certain kinds of food, accept it and never mention it again. Then, there are people who cannot let it go, who will say that if I try their salmon dish or shrimp-something that I will love it.

I shake my head. "Can you just let it go?"

He shrugs, turning his attention toward my suitcase. "All right, open her up. Let's see what you have."

"Huh?"

"This is your first trip overseas, right?"

I nod.

"I want to make sure you haven't forgotten anything."

My mouth drops. "I'm fine. Thanks."

What does he think I am, some little kid? I push the picture of my mom helping me pack out of my mind. I've only read every travel guide known to man in the last three months. I'm probably better packed than he is. Besides, I don't want him seeing my underwear or my stockpile of tampons.

He nods, lifting his hands. "Only trying to help."

I wrinkle my nose.

He stands, walking over to the fridge and grabs another beer. "If you don't want my help, that's cool."

"I'm fine. Thanks for the offer."

On his way back to the couch, he pauses by my bag to lift it. I start to say something, but he puts it back down before I can.

"Have you weighed it already?"

I nod. "It's under fifty pounds."

As he sits he's looking at it, not me. He smiles and tips his drink back. I watch his throat move as he swallows. I gulp. He glances over at me. I look away, picking up my soda, and I take a sip.

He leans back, stretching his arm across the back of the couch, his body facing me. "So, other than the eating stuff, what should I know about you?"

I tilt my head to the side. "What do you mean?"

He smirks. "What do you want out of this trip?"

I look down at my hands and randomly pick at the remnants of my last nail polish job. "I'm—"

His phone rings, interrupting me. He looks down at the screen before standing. "I have to take this," he says, walking to the door.

I'm alone in his apartment. His call is important enough to take in the hallway. The stairwell amplifies his voice. I can almost hear every word he's saying. I stand, moving over to my suitcase that is closer to the door, to listen in.

"I'm leaving the keys with Mr. Wiltshire. Yeah, we leave tomorrow morning."

There's a pause, and I hear his footsteps. It sounds like he's pacing.

"Some girl." There's a pause. "Yeah, she's never even been outside of the U.S. Hopefully, she won't slow me down. All I know is that her parents are paying." Another pause. "She's probably spoiled."

My heart stops. Is he talking about me? I blink away the sting I feel in my eyes. I can't believe he just said that. He doesn't even know me. How alone I feel in that moment hits me. I wish I could talk to Ally. She would know what to do. A tear slides down my cheek, and I push it away with the back of my hand.

With my pale skin, it's impossible to hide when I cry. My eyes get puffy, and my face gets splotchy. I pull out my toiletry bag, a travel one with a built-in hook to hang on the back of a door. I march over to the door and crack it.

"Hang on a sec," he says into the phone.

"I'm going to take my shower," I huff. Then, I close the door before he has a chance to respond.

I don't need him, I think to myself, taking my
toiletry bag and some clothes to sleep in as I head
to the bathroom.

There is a shelf with clean towels in the corner
of the bathroom. I grab one and set it on the toilet
before I start the shower and hang my bag from a
hook on the back of the bathroom door. His
bathroom doesn't have a fan or a window to vent
the steam. I quickly undress and step under the
spray. I like my showers hot, borderline scalding. It
takes a minute to get used to, but then it feels
heavenly.

I use some of Adam's shampoo, not wanting to
waste any of mine. He has plain old Head &
Shoulders 2-in-1. His soap is Irish Spring. I lather
my washcloth, holding it up to my nose and
inhaling before washing myself.

It feels weird, showering in a boy's bathroom.
I might be more excited about it if I hadn't just
heard him call me spoiled. It still feels fun to touch
his things. He has a razor and shaving cream in
here. Using my own razor, I borrow some cream
to touch up my legs and bikini line. As I rinse the
shampoo out of my hair, I wonder more about
Adam. Does he ever jerk off in here? It makes me
feel warm, just thinking about it.

I turn off the water and towel off. I pull on an
old T-shirt and shorts to sleep in before wrapping
the towel around my head. I crack the door to let

the steam out, and I jump when Adam pulls it open the rest of the way.

"Any hot water left?" he asks, batting away some steam in front of him.

I shrug and reach past him to grab my toothbrush from my bag. He doesn't move, and my arm grazes his shoulder. He unnerves me. I'm annoyed at myself for still being attracted to him even after hearing what he said about me. Just because he looks good doesn't mean he's a nice person.

I want to seem unaffected, so I pointedly ignore him. I use his toothpaste, not wanting to reach past him again. He leans against the doorframe and watches me brush my teeth. I do it as neatly as possible. Then, I rinse my mouth daintily instead of just spitting like I would if he wasn't watching me.

I unwrap the towel from my head and use it to squeeze any excess water I can from my hair. When my hair was long, it was a production to brush, dry, and add leave in conditioner to it. My hair is short enough now that I don't have to brush it.

The steam clears from the mirror. I lean forward to part my hair with my fingers, sweeping my long bangs to the side. I didn't want to be the first to say anything, but I'm running out of things to do, and he's still just standing there.

I sigh. "Let me get out of your way."

His mouth twitches. There's a long pause where we're just standing there, staring at each other, before he nods. I turn and drape my towel over the rod. I grab my dirty clothes, leaving my other things where they are, so I can use them in the morning.

He steps back to let me pass, but his apartment is so tight that I'm still almost chest-to-chest with him. Part of me wishes I had put on a sports bra. Moving past him without one on leaves me feeling exposed.

I have an interior travel bag just for socks and undies. I leave my jeans out, deciding I'll just wear them again tomorrow. The shirt I wore today is fine to be worn again, just on another day. Rule number one in traveling around the world is that clothes can go multiple wears between washes. I refold and pack it. I pull out a simple gray long-sleeved shirt since it'll probably be cold on the plane. I also have a black scarf in my carry-on that can double as a light mini blanket.

The breath that I hadn't realized I was holding escapes when I hear the shower turn on. I sag back against the sofa, noticing that Adam has already put sheets and a blanket on it. The idea of already being in bed and asleep, whether I'm faking it or not, is a welcome one.

I sit back up and rummage through my bag in search of a bottle of lotion. It's institutional-sized. My skin is on the dry side normally, and traveling only makes it worse. It's an old habit to smooth some on after my shower. My mom even found this travel-safe bottle for it from a catalog. The lid resembles a childproof cover from a pill bottle.

I haven't gotten the trick down yet to open it without trying a couple of times. Maybe if I hadn't been fighting with it, I would have noticed that the shower stopped. Instead, as I'm smoothing lotion over my legs, I feel the hairs on the back of my neck prick up with the sensation that I'm being watched.

I'm sitting on the sofa, and my back is toward the bathroom door. It finally dawns on me that I can't hear the shower anymore. My body stills. I want to turn my head. I know he is somewhere behind me, but I need to finish rubbing the lotion in, or I run the risk of having goopy legs. So, I ignore him and finish rubbing the lotion on my legs before I put some on my arms.

I can hear him moving around—a closet door opens, the sound of a drawer, and the rustle of clothes. I'm thankful my back is toward him when I feel my face redden.

"Why is your neck all red?"

Shit. Damn fair skin. If my hair were still long, he wouldn't have been able to see that.

"It is?" I hedge, turning to face him.

Damn. My tongue suddenly feels too small for my mouth. I have to resist the urge to let it hang out while I pant.

Adam, still damp from his shower, is standing by a closet next to the front door. He's not wearing a shirt, and I'm finding it impossible to not stare at his chest. He's beautiful. It's impossible to ignore the definition of his muscles so clear on his lightly tanned skin.

There's a ceiling light behind him that catches the tiny beads of water clinging to the tips of his hair, giving him a strange halo. It also makes it hard to see the expression on his face. I watch, transfixed, as one bead of water expands and then falls from his hair to the top of his shoulder.

I don't even know him, and I want to lick it off of him. I gulp and turn away, fiddling with the cap of my lotion bottle until it is on right. It doesn't help that my fingers are still slick.

I stand and pause when I feel light-headed before moving past him to where my bag is. I dump the lotion bottle on top of my bag before moving back to the couch.

I push the sheet and blanket back. "I'm going to…"

I gesture to the sofa, and he nods, freeing more tiny beads of water to fall from his hair.

"I'm setting the alarm for five. The cab will be here at six. That enough time for you?"

My back is to him, but I can hear him opening the cabinet with his bed. The hinges groan as he slowly lowers it to the ground behind me.

"Sounds good," I manage.

It's hard to concentrate. From where the cabinet hiding his Murphy bed is to where the couch is, it's like we're sharing one large bed with a small gap between them. It would feel less awkward if my head were at the opposite end of the couch, but it's not.

The only thing keeping me from being perfectly lined up to him is the small end table between the wall and the couch. Instead of being even with his face if I turned over, I'd probably be level with his abs. It is much safer to sleep with my back to any of that tonight.

EIGHT

I squeeze my eyes shut and try to burrow myself under the blanket as a strong hand shakes my shoulder.

"Five more minutes," I mumble.

I hear a chuckle behind me before he says, "No can do," and he pulls the blanket off of me.

I reach in vain for it, but he's too fast, so I cover my face with my arm and try to tuck myself into the back of the couch.

"C'mon, Aubrey. The cab is going to be here soon."

It takes me a moment to remember where I am. I lift my head, turning it to look back at Adam, and I squint at him with one eye. His Murphy bed is already put away, and he's already dressed, looking too annoyingly put together this early in the morning.

I turn the rest of the way, sliding my legs out, until they fall off the sofa, and I use my arm to hoist myself up into a sitting position. I've never been much of a morning person. It usually takes me some time to fully wake up.

I blink at him for a minute, and then I yawn, narrowing my eyes at him when I see one corner of his mouth briefly pull up. I'm tired. I don't feel like amusing anyone. I tilt my head to the side and wince at how stiff it feels. His couch is deep, but I must have slept weird on it anyway.

I roll my head a couple of times as I rub my neck, too tired to care that he's watching me. I stand, walking over to my bag to grab my clothes for today, and I head to the bathroom.

I laugh when I see my reflection. The ribbing from the pillow I used last night has left its mark across my cheek, and my hair seems to be defying gravity on one side as it concaves on the other. I ignore it and change first, feeling more clothed the second I have a bra on.

Once I'm dressed, I tackle my hair. Deciding to wet it and let it dry all over again is the safest way to go. I brush my teeth and wash my face. I don't wear much makeup normally, but I swear by tinted moisturizer.

Once I'm ready, I repack all of my toiletries and walk out. Adam looks surprised that I got ready so fast.

Ha, I think to myself, remembering last night when he told someone I was spoiled.

It still bugs me. He doesn't even know me. I kneel in front of my suitcase and check and then double-check it before wrapping my TSA-approved strap-style lock around it.

"That's some lock," he says, leaning over me.

I shrug. "My mom found it in some catalog."

I flip my backpack over and rummage through it for my watch.

"Are those solar panels?"

I glance up at him. "Cool, huh? My mom found it—"

"In a catalog," he finishes, one corner of his mouth pulling up.

I nod. Once I've found my watch, I put it on. It's crazy high-tech. It has time zones, temperatures, multiple alarm settings, and other stuff I haven't figured out yet. I have the manual to read on the plane. The only problem with it is that it's huge, dwarfing my wrist. I cover it with the sleeve of my gray shirt and stand.

"We can grab some breakfast at the café across the street and wait for the cab."

I nod, pulling my backpack on before I stand. I reach for my bag, but he pushes my hand away, picking it up himself.

"You don't have to do that," I argue.

"It's cool," he mumbles, motioning with his head for me to go ahead of him.

I hold the door open for him. He moves past me, setting our bags down on the landing, before locking the door behind us. He pulls an envelope out from the back pocket of his jeans and drops the key in it. Then, he slides the envelope under his neighbor's door before picking our bags back up and making his way down the stairs.

I walk behind him, my eyes glued to the ridges of his biceps straining against the fabric of his shirt. I'm not paying attention to my feet, and I grab the railing before I stumble into him. When he glances back, I'm innocently inspecting the ceiling molding, purposely avoiding his eyes.

I take over pulling my suitcase once we're on the ground floor. He holds the door for me, and then I follow him across the street to a small sidewalk café.

"What do you want?" he asks, setting his suitcase next to a bistro-style table.

"You don't have to buy me breakfast." I slip my bag off of one shoulder, so I can swing it around in front of me. My wallet is in it.

He waves his hand. "George will kick my ass if I let you pay."

I zip my bag shut and shrug it off before hanging it on the back of my chair. I sit down and look at the chalkboard-style menu on the wall.

"Can I get a bacon and egg sandwich with an orange juice?"

He nods, taking off his backpack and setting it on his chair, before going to place our orders. He walks back with two cups a minute later.

"Not a coffee drinker?" he asks, passing me a cup.

"I drink coffee, just not every day," I say before taking a sip of my drink.

He moves his bag from his chair to the ground and sits. "George will bring the food out in a sec."

I look away and take another sip of my juice.

"Didn't you say you needed caffeine or a shower to wake up?" he asks, gesturing to my cup.

I point to my still damp hair. "Sink bath."

He nods, and then he turns as a man carrying a tray comes up next to our table.

"So, this is your travel companion?"

Adam's face breaks into a wide grin. I stare at his teeth. He could advertise toothpaste.

"George, this is Aubrey. Aubrey, this is George. George and I grew up together."

I look up and smile at George. He's on the round side and shorter than Adam, but he seems nice. He sets our food on the table and pulls another chair over to sit with us.

I've just taken a bite when he says to Adam, "You didn't mention that she's so pretty."

My eyes flick to Adam's as I try to swallow my bite without choking. His eyes meet mine.

"That's because I just met her last night."

"Where are you guys heading to first?"

It's his friend, so I focus on my sandwich and let him do the talking. George leaves after a minute when his boss shouts for him to get back to work. Adam checks his watch before eating his sandwich in two bites. He washes it down with the rest of his coffee.

"Hurry up," he orders, sounding like my dad. "The cab will be here any second."

I narrow my eyes at him, but I don't say anything as I finish my breakfast. He better not be so bossy the whole trip.

I've just finished when the cab pulls up. He takes our trash and dumps it in a can before waving at the cabbie. I'm putting on my backpack as he grabs both of our suitcases and makes his way back across the street. I give a half wave to George before jogging after Adam. My head is still turned, and I jump when a car honks at me.

I mouth, *Sorry*, and dash the rest of the way across the street.

"Be careful," Adam snaps when I reach him.

I step around him and climb into the cab. I pull my bag into my lap and pout. He didn't need to grouch at me. When he climbs in on the other side, I pointedly look out my window.

"You kids going to JFK, right?" the cabbie confirms.

"Yep," Adam replies.

My hand is on the seat between us. I shift it closer to the back of the seat and bump into Adam's hand. I glance down at our hands before I pick mine up and cross my arms, which is dumb because I slide into him at the first turn.

"God, sorry," I mumble.

Adam laughs, pushing me off himself. I hold on to the door handle the rest of the ride.

Adam pays the cabbie when we get to the airport. I offer, but he just shakes his head. He walks quickly inside, and I struggle to keep up with him. A couple of times, he looks back at me like he's annoyed.

"Asshole," I mumble under my breath before I catch up with him.

The line to check-in is long, but it moves quickly. I move my suitcase between myself and the pushy lady behind me after she hits the back of my foot twice. It moves me closer to Adam, and the look he gives—like he thinks I'm doing it for him—annoys me.

When the line moves again, I purposely leave a good-sized gap between us. When Adam walks up to the counter agent, he motions for me to follow him. He puts his hand out for my ticket and passport. I pause before handing them to him, not really sure why I couldn't have just handed them to the lady myself.

Once we're checked in, I have to jog to keep up with him as we head to the security check section. I'm annoyed with him, so I pick a different line than him. He rolls his eyes at me as he takes off his shoes. I mentally will my line to move faster than his, so I can beat him. It doesn't. In fact, my line takes way longer.

I avoid his eyes when I walk over to where he's waiting for me. He doesn't say anything. He just turns and starts walking toward our gate.

I don't even try to keep up with him. There are too many people, and we have plenty of time to get to our gate. When I finally get there, I look around for him. He bobs his head up when my eyes find him. His bag is on the seat next to him. He moves it when I walk up.

"Thanks," I mumble, sinking into the seat.

"I lost you back there."

I glance at him. "You walk too fast for me."

He has the decency to look embarrassed. "You should have said something."

I shrug. "I caught up."

"True, but it's rude. I'm sorry."

My mouth drops. "You don't have to apologize for walking fast."

He shakes his head. "I'm supposed to be looking out for you."

"I'm not a kid. I don't need a babysitter," I grumble.

His mouth twitches before he looks away.

I reach into my bag for my watch manual.

"What are you reading?" he asks, leaning over my shoulder.

I move away from him, and I press the manual to my chest, so he won't see it. "Nothing."

"Is that a manual?" he asks, trying to lift one of my fingers.

I close my eyes and hand it to him, doing my best to ignore his chuckle. My eyes are still closed when he sets it back down on my lap. My eyes flick open, and I shove the manual back into my bag.

"That's a thick manual for a watch." He picks up my hand and pushes my sleeve back to look at it. "That thing is huge. It'd be big on my wrist."

I tug my arm back and pull my sleeve down to cover my watch. "Chunky watches are in right now."

One corner of his mouth pulls up. "Did your mom find it in a catalog?"

I can't help but smile. "Maybe," I admit.

We start boarding not long after. Adam has an aisle seat, so I'll have to climb over him every time I need to get up. Great.

On the other side of me is a pretty blonde. She gets an eyeful of Adam and immediately starts a conversation with him over me. The worst part is that he lets her. She leans on the armrest between our seats, her cleavage millimeters from my arm. He doesn't seem to mind.

This is not how I pictured this moment. I wanted a chance to reflect and think about Ally. I needed to feel her and have her still be a part of this journey. What I did not need was boobs in my face.

"Do you want me to switch seats with you?" I grit once we're in the air.

"No, I'm good. Did you want the aisle?"

I smirk at him. "I just thought you might enjoy your conversation better if you were sitting here."

He smirks. "That so?"

"Do you two know each other?" she asks.

I smile tightly and answer honestly, "Not really."

Then, I pull out my watch manual to read while I ignore them. I put it away after I have successfully set the time zone for home. I pull out headphones, so I can watch a movie, and I am surprised when Adam does the same.

"Which one are you going to watch?" he asks.

We each have our own screen mounted into the seat in front of us. There is a menu of movies and TV shows available. I shrug as I scroll through them. I was going to watch a chick flick, but I am embarrassed to admit it. I feel like he would judge my choice, so I decide to watch a crime drama instead.

"I'll watch it with you," Adam says, putting his headphones on and touching his screen to get to the same movie.

"Watch what you want to watch."

"I don't like watching movies alone," he says as he scrolls through the menu.

"But we'll both be wearing headphones," I argue.

He shrugs, pulling up the same movie that's on my screen. He reaches across me and presses the button to start both screens at the same time. The girl in the seat next to mine fumbles with her screen, trying to catch up with ours. I don't know why this makes me happy, but it does. I like that he didn't set up her screen.

During a particularly suspenseful scene, I jump. I glance over at Adam and catch him trying not to laugh.

Whatever, I think to myself. *I'm totally watching that chick flick next.*

A stewardess comes around to pass out drinks, and again not long after with lunch. After the stewardess comes back around to clear our trash, I pause my movie, and Adam stops his as well.

"You can keep watching. I was just going to go use the restroom."

He unbuckles his belt. "I'll go with you."

"I can go to the restroom by myself. I promise, I won't get lost," I joke.

"I know that. I might also need to go."

I can't argue with that logic. He stands, moving back, to let me walk in front of him. I use the tops of the seats to keep my balance as I walk. I've never been good at walking on a plane.

When I get to the restrooms, I grimace. There's a line. The guy in front of me turns his head back to look at me, and he smiles. I give a polite closed-mouth smile back and jump when Adam comes up close behind me. The guy in front of me sees him and turns his head back around. I glare at Adam.

He ignores my look and nonchalantly says, "Tight squeeze back here," to excuse how close he's standing next to me. "So, what do you think of the movie?"

I lean against the wall. "That part with the dog freaked me out."

His mouth twitches. "I noticed."

I turn to face him. "So, why didn't you want to switch seats? I think that girl is interested in you."

He looks up at the ceiling. "I'm not interested in her."

I'm curious. "Why not?"

His gray eyes meet mine. "Just not."

I tilt my head. "Well, that clears it up."

I see the line has moved, and I take another step forward. Adam follows me even though no one is behind him. Two doors open at the same time.

I look at him. "Race you."

Why did I say that? I wonder.

I don't really want to race. I just want to go to the restroom and not trip or fall walking back to my seat. When I open the door, Adam is waiting there for me.

"I won," is all he says before walking back toward our seats.

I roll my eyes and follow him. He stands there, waiting for me, so I can sit first. I try not to laugh when I notice the girl next to us paused her movie as well.

I slip my headphones back on. He starts both of our movies at the same time again. I check my watch and groan when I realize we aren't even halfway yet. He must have noticed.

He's looking at me and mouths, *Okay?*

I nod and look back at the screen.

After the movie, the girl next to us produces a deck of cards, and we play poker for a while. I so catch Adam sneaking a peek at my hand more than once. I watch my chick flick when playing cards gets boring. I'm a little surprised when Adam decides to watch as well, and I'm less surprised when the girl does too.

This movie is hotter than I expected. I start feeling flushed after a couple of scenes, and I turn my fan on. I catch Adam suppressing a smile out of the corner of my eye. I wonder if scenes like this affect guys the same way or if they need more nudity.

I find myself watching him out of the corner of my eye during the steamy parts. I look at him again, only to find him watching me.

NINE

I snap my eyes forward in an attempt to play off that he just caught me. I try to get back into the movie, but instead, I'm hyperaware of his presence next to me. I'm fighting an internal battle against sneaking another glance at him.

I don't get why I'm having this type of reaction to him. He's good-looking, but there's something else, something I can't explain. In moments like these, when I'm not actively disliking him, I feel a pull to him. We'll be circling the globe together, and the sensation I feel toward Adam is almost gravitational.

I wish I could get a read on him. He's done nice things for me, but he has also been a dick. I get that he's here to look out for me, but it really pisses me off when he gets bossy. Like last night, when he wanted to inspect my luggage. What was that about? Then, today, walking all fast, not even paying attention to if I could keep up. Total jerk move. Yes, he apologized, but it was still annoying. It's hard to stay angry though when he does stuff like buy me breakfast or carry my bag.

It just doesn't seem smart to crush on him, considering I'll be stuck with him for the next two months. Besides, this trip is supposed to be about finding myself and Ally. What kind of niece am I to already be so distracted? He is Captain Distraction.

I'm so wrapped up in my brain that I don't notice the movie has ended until Adam reaches up to stop it, making the credits disappear.

"So, what did you think?"

I slip off the headphones. "It was okay," I answer noncommittally. Then, I look at him. "What about you?"

He slowly wraps the cord around his headphones and pauses, hands still in midair. "I thought it was total bullshit."

The force of his answer catches me off guard. "Why?"

He loops the cord the last few times around and bends to tuck them into the front pocket of his bag. "There is no way a misunderstanding like that would get so blown out of proportion. All that girl had to do was tell him the truth."

I nod, thinking I must have missed that part because I have no idea what he is talking about.

The girl on the other side of me disagrees. "She was just waiting for the right time."

"That's bullshit," I mutter, cringing when I realize I said that out loud.

They both stare at me, so I shrug.

"That's just an excuse to put off doing something you don't want to do."

She keeps going, saying something about a dog. I stop listening, and I find myself wondering how Herman is doing in his new home. Does he miss me? I know it's a good thing that he got adopted since the idea of him being in a kennel and not being able to visit him bugs me.

I'm still half listening to them argue when I feel my ears pop. The touch screen in front of me has an option to watch the flight path of the plane. It also shows our altitude. I work my jaw in an effort to relieve the pressure in my ears.

"Gum?" Adam asks, holding out a piece.

"What flavor is it?"

"Not seafood," he teases.

I make a face. "That's just gross. Come on, what kind is it?"

He smirks. "I don't know. It's some kind of peppermint."

"Sure," I say, plucking it from his fingers.

"Is there a flavor you would have said no to?"

I watch the altitude drop again on the screen. "I don't like the cinnamon kind. Why?"

He taps the side of his head. "Just adding it to the list."

"Har-har. I'm sure there are things you don't like to eat."

He blinks a couple of times as he thinks about it. "I don't like overly sweet things but"—he lifts a brow— "I can eat them if I need to." He bumps his shoulder into mine. "It helps to be flexible when traveling."

I nod halfheartedly. The girl next to me uses this as an opportunity to tell Adam all the different kinds of foods she likes.

I can't handle it, so I put my headphones back on and find a radio station. The songs are awful, but it's still better than talking about food. The only problem is since we're landing soon, there are more announcements from the crew, announcements that blare full volume into the headphones on my ears. After the second one, I pull off my headphones and put them in my bag.

Adam pauses, like he's going to say something to me, only he doesn't.

When we land, the girl next to us asks what our plans are in London and how long we'll be in town. I know she's saying *you guys*, but her questions are clearly directed to Adam, not me.

He avoids her eyes, "Just staying overnight. We're headed to Belgium tomorrow."

He's lying. We're going to be in London for at least three days.

I avoid looking at him. It bothers me how convincing he is when he says it. Is he scared he'll hurt her feelings if he says he doesn't want to see her while we're in town? She's just some random girl on a plane. If he could lie so easily over something so trivial, can I even trust him?

She's still undeterred and offers him her business card. I feel bad for her and envy her all at the same time. She's brave, and that's one thing I want to be.

We are separated from her as we make our way through customs. For some reason, I'm nervous once it's my turn to get my passport stamped. As if I've forgotten I'm actually an international drug smuggler, and they're on to me. I'm also not thrilled with my passport picture. The lighting was weird at the pharmacy where I had it taken. I look even paler than normal, and my hair wasn't cooperating that day. When the officer does a double take, I can only hope it's because I don't look that bad in real life.

While we wait for the baggage claim carousel to spring to life, I look around for the girl who sat next to me.

When I don't see her, I turn to Adam. "Why did you lie to that girl?"

"What?"

I glance around for her again. "You know, that girl who was sitting next to me. Why did you tell her we are leaving tomorrow?"

He shrugged. "I had a feeling she wouldn't take the hint. If she had known we were going to be here for a couple of days, I think she'd want to meet up."

"Why didn't you just tell her you weren't interested?" I ask, inching closer to the belt.

His movements mirror mine. "You don't think that would have been harsh?"

I look at my feet. "I don't think lying was any better."

I watch as he shuffles his feet.

"I don't see the point in hurting the feelings of some girl I'm never going to see again."

I don't even know why it's bugging me as much as it is. I understand what he's saying. I just don't like that he did it.

We both jump when a hand clamps down on Adam's shoulder. When he turns, his face breaks into a wide grin. I stand there while Adam hugs and greets some guy.

"Abe, this is Aubrey."

I put my hand out, but instead, I'm also pulled into a hug. Abe is so tall that it feels like my face is pressed against his stomach. The wool of his blue sweater itches my cheek.

Once I'm released, we stand together and watch the parade of luggage before us. Adam's bag comes first, and mine is not too far behind. Abe pulls my bag for me, and I trail after them to the exit.

Abe has quite a stride, given his long limbs. I fear falling behind, like I did in New York. Instead, I can tell Adam is walking slower than before, causing Abe to slow down as well. I listen to their conversation as we make our way to Abe's car. Or his mother's car. Or his mother's sister's car.

112

Something like that. He borrowed it from someone to come to collect us.

It's fun to watch Abe fold himself into such a small car. He has the driver's seat pushed all the way back, but his knees still come up a bit on either side of the steering wheel.

It's not until we're on the road that it strikes me that I'm in another country. The sensation of driving on the other side of the road is odd, especially during right turns. It just doesn't feel right.

Abe is also a fairly aggressive driver. He gets right on the bumper of the car in front of us and has no issue using his horn to make his presence known.

Abe shares a place with another roommate, who is on holiday. There is, it turns out, some confusion on Abe's part as to my relationship with Adam. He assumes we'll just share his mate's bed.

Adam glances back at me while Abe parks. "Don't worry. Aubrey likes lumpy couches."

I discreetly look out the window to avoid his gray gaze. I think back to last night, how the thought of sleeping in his bed affected me. To now be in a car with one of his friends who thought we were a couple. The idea does funny things to my stomach, or maybe it's just my reaction to the car no longer moving.

Adam holds the front seat down while I hoist myself out of the bucket-style backseat. I ease myself past him, purposely avoiding touching him.

While Adam's place is a minimalist's dream, Abe's apartment is a stale cigarette–smelling, cluttered mess. I take one look at the stained couch and glance at Adam. His mouth twitches like he wants to laugh.

How can he think this is funny? Shouldn't he be breaking out in hives just from being here?

Our bags are both in the main room. I'm trying to figure out how to claim the bedroom when Abe asks if I'm hungry.

I nod. "I can eat."

Adam walks past me to look at something on a bookshelf. "Fish and chips?"

"Okay—" Abe starts.

Adam stops him. "Aubrey, will you eat fish and chips?"

Asshole. I give him the same answer as the night before. "Sure, just hold the fish."

I walk over to my bag and tilt my head toward Abe. "Which room is your roommate's?"

He gestures past me. I snap the handle up and walk into the room, closing the door behind me. I'm sure that doesn't make me a great guest, but Adam is annoying, and I need a moment to myself.

Abe's roommate's room turns out to be cleaner than the other parts of the apartment I have seen. The bed is made. I pull the sheets back and sniff them, exhaling with relief that they smell fresh. I flop down onto the bed, careful to let my feet hang off the edge.

I turn my head toward the door when I hear a knock. "Come in."

It's Adam. He opens the door and leans against the frame. "Are you mad?"

I hear my dad's voice in my head, and his words come out of my mouth. "People don't get mad. Animals do."

"So, if you aren't mad, what are you?" He smirks.

I deliberately turn my face away from him. "Are you going to make fun of me about what I eat everywhere we go?

I hear the door close and then his footsteps as he moves closer to the bed. I flip over when I feel the mattress accommodate his weight as he sits on the edge of the bed. His back is to me.

He leans forward, putting his elbows on his knees and his head in his hands. "I'm not trying to be a dick."

I want to tell him he's failing. Instead, I say nothing.

"Are you going to talk to me?" He turns his head back to look at me.

I sniff and look up at the ceiling. "Will you stop it with the food stuff?"

I hear him exhale.

"I was only joking."

Now, I feel bad for making it a big deal. "I'm just sensitive about it. I don't care what other people do or don't eat. I don't understand why it's a big deal what I do."

"Not another word. I promise."

I roll to the other side of the bed to get up. "I am hungry."

He stands too, turning to face me. He almost smiles. "Let's see what we can do to fix that."

I follow him out of the room, still happy I staked my claim on it.

Abe is snacking on Skips. He rolls the bag shut and tosses it onto the kitchen counter. "We ready?"

Adam glances back at me and nods. "What's good around here?"

Abe looks at Adam, then me, and then back at Adam. "There's a pizza place nearby. The pizza is more okay than good, but it's close. We can walk and go to the pub after."

Adam looks at me. "Pizza sound good?"

I nod and dash back into the room to grab a cross-body purse from my suitcase, and I put my wallet in it. Adam and Abe are waiting for me by the door.

As we walk to the pizza place, Abe talks animatedly about his new camera or maybe a new lens. The name is a combo of letters and numbers. Adam seems to understand what he's talking about. He asks to see it later.

I follow them, noticing Adam still slows his stride, so I don't have to run to keep up with them. The pizza place is on the corner of the next street.

We're quickly seated and order. It isn't long before we're served. The promptness of the staff may be the only positive thing about the place. It might be the worst pizza I have ever had. The cheese tastes stale. I'm hungry though, so I manage to finish my slice. I can't help but notice Adam regarding his slice warily before eating it.

The pub we go to next is back toward Abe's flat. It is small, dark, and crowded. I ask for a light ale. I don't know what the different brands are, other than Guinness, which I already know is too heavy for me. I'm not much of a beer drinker in general. I prefer sweet, fruity, frozen drinks. Those, unfortunately, are not on the menu.

Adam passes me a glass full of a wheat-colored draft. I take a tentative test sip.

"You like it?" He watches for my reaction.

I lick my lips. "Yeah, thanks. What is it?"

"It's a Freedom Pilsner."

I lift my glass. "To freedom!"

He presses his lips together, and Abe laughs as we toast. I sip my drink, thinking its name is weirdly fitting for my journey.

Abe finds us a small table with two chairs. He takes one, and I take the other. Adam stands between us, his hand tilting his glass. I stare at his hand, curious about why he's doing that. He sets his glass down, and I look up at him. He's watching me. I break our gaze and take a drink, randomly looking around the bar.

There's a guy standing with a group not far from us. He's handsome in that classic broad-shouldered, strong jaw way. He lifts his glass and smiles at me. I glance back to make sure no one is behind me just to be sure before I smile back. I feel my face get hot as he leaves his friends and walks over to our table.

"Hi, I'm Nigel," he says, offering his hand to me.

Adam's talking to Abe and misses Nigel's approach. Adam gives Nigel a confused look, and then Adam sees me smile at Nigel as I shake his hand. Adam rolls his eyes and starts to open his mouth, but I kick him under the table. His eyes flash. He pushes off the table and crosses his arms over his chest, smirking.

I ignore Adam as best I can. "I'm Aubrey."

Nigel smiles. "Are you American?"

I nod. "Yes."

"On a holiday?" He leans against the table, so he's between Adam and me.

Adam is taller than Nigel, and he watches us over his shoulder.

I tell Nigel that I am, and trying not to be rude, I attempt to introduce Nigel to Adam and Abe. Nigel halfway turns and waves at them before facing me again. I press my lips together to avoid laughing at the expressions on both Adam's and Abe's faces.

"Are you in town for long?"

I cringe. "Just a couple of days."

He leans in, his face close to mine. "Need a tour guide?"

I can't help but giggle when Adam's mouth drops.

"That's really nice of you to offer, but I'm all set." I gesture to Adam and Abe.

Undeterred, Nigel hands me a business card. "My mobile number is on the back if you change your mind."

I watch him walk back over to his friends. When he gets to them, he looks back at me and winks. I play it cool as best I can by nodding, and then I pretend to be really absorbed by the poster on the wall behind Abe.

"Well, what do you think of that?" Abe asks Adam.

He shrugs. "You could have said yes to that guy."

"I know," I snap. "Why? You think I thought I needed your permission?"

He blinks. "I didn't say that."

"Right," I say before finishing my drink.

He shakes his head and walks over to the bar to get another round. I gruffly thank him when he returns and passes me my glass.

"No big deal." He glances over to where Nigel is standing.

I wonder if he was talking about Nigel or the drink. "Either way, I can buy the next."

He looks over at Abe and then back at me. "We're probably going to take off after this one. You can buy tomorrow night."

"Oh." I look down at the table and run the pad of my index finger along the ribbed lip of the table.

"Did you want to stay longer?"

I shake my head. It makes sense that we are leaving soon. We have a full day of sightseeing planned for tomorrow. I was being silly. It's just that it's my first night in London. I'm underwhelmed so far.

The planning of this trip consumed me for the last several months, so I might have unrealistic expectations of what to expect. It's probably the time difference. It's late. It just doesn't feel late yet. I focus on finishing my drink, and I half listen to Abe talk about his recent trip to Germany.

Adam and I walk side by side on the way to Abe's flat. Abe is behind us, having what sounds like an argument with his girlfriend over the phone. He passes Adam his keys and stays downstairs to finish his conversation.

I grab my bath stuff and go to wash my face and brush my teeth. When I walk back into my room, I jump when I see Adam in there.

TEN

"What are you doing in here?" I stammer.

He's on his knees by the bed, reaching under. "This bed is a trundle. There's no way I'm sleeping on that sofa."

"But I'm sleeping in here," I argue.

I watch as he pulls out the trundle. It's smaller, maybe twin-sized.

"Yes, and I'm sleeping here." He makes a wide sweep with his hands over the smaller bed.

I remember how awkward it felt, sleeping so near him the night before. At least the trundle is low to the ground.

My mouth drops as he depresses a lever and raises it to the same height as my bed, and the way it's made, we'll be face-to-face with maybe an inch separating his bed from mine.

I gulp. He turns to look at me.

"Um, I was going to get changed."

"Oh, don't mind me."

"Out," I order him.

His eyes travel lazily down me, and I shiver. One corner of his mouth pulls up before he turns to leave, closing the door behind him. I hurry over to it and lock it, sagging against it. I was looking forward to a night away from him. I quickly change, unlock the door, and climb into bed. I hear the door open, and I shuffle farther under the covers.

When I awake the next morning, I'm facing him. Wiping sleep from my eyes, I watch him. He's shirtless, his sheet draping low across his hips. I lick my lips, mesmerized by the rise and fall of his chest. I quietly slip out of bed and out of the room, taking my clothes for the day with me.

I need distance. I can't stay in that room any longer. It smells like him—a mixture of Irish Spring, his cologne, and something just him.

I shower and get dressed. I'm in the kitchen, rummaging through the cabinets for something to snack on, when he walks out. He's still shirtless. Why can't he put on a shirt?

"Hungry?" he asks, scratching the back of his head.

"A bit," I admit.

"Give me a minute. I saw a bakery close by."

"Okay."

He walks back into the room and shuts the door. A couple of minutes later, he walks back out, now in jeans and a vintage looking *M*A*S*H* T-shirt.

"Nice shirt."

He laughs. "It was my dad's."

"You're wearing hand-me-downs?" I joke.

"Just trying to live the green life."

I don't give him the satisfaction of a chuckle even though that was funny as I follow him out of the flat.

"What about Abe?"

"He can get his own breakfast," he says, grabbing a set of keys hanging on a hook by the door.

I give him a look.

"Don't worry. I'll bring him something back." He holds the door open for me.

I tuck my hair behind my ear and hurry down the stairs. I wait for him at the bottom, not sure which direction to go. He comes up beside me, tilting his head to the right. We turn together and walk.

"I saw you."

"Excuse me?" I stop.

He's now a step ahead of me. He looks back at me.

"I saw you watching me this morning."

"I wasn't," I stammer, looking away.

"If you say so," he says as he continues to walk.

I follow him but stay a step behind on purpose. I can't believe he saw me. I'm not sure if I've ever been so embarrassed. I might never be able to look him in the eyes again. It's a short walk to the bakery. Adam orders some assorted pastries and two coffees.

"Do you think Abe would like one too?" I ask as he passes me my cup.

He shakes his head. "He drinks tea."

"Tea?" I picture my grandmother and her floral teapot.

He shrugs. "It's a British thing."

"Yeah, Boston Tea Party and all that, I suppose."

His mouth twitches.

I try to follow him again, but he slows to walk next to me. I sip my coffee and instead watch the cars pass by. The street Abe lives on is a one-way. I see where he parked the car he picked us up in. The street is so packed that I'm surprised he was able to find a spot so close.

"See something interesting?"

My eyes flick to Adam's and then down. How interesting will I sound when I tell him I was thinking about how Abe got a good parking spot? I shake my head.

Since Adam's hands are full, I hold the door for him this time. He rests his foot against the door, tilting his chin toward the stairs. I'm not sure if he's polite or bossy. The idea of the chivalrous male is sometimes annoying. It sounds good in theory, and if my hands are full, it doesn't bug me.

I let out a puff of air and try to temper my feet from stomping. Once I'm at Abe's door, I lean against the wall next to it, not offering to help.

Adam holds the bag with the pastries in his mouth as he reaches in his pocket for the keys. He's fumbling with them, trying to isolate the right one, when the door opens.

"Yum." Abe grins, plucking the bag from Adam's mouth.

We crowd around his coffee table. Adam and I both sit on the floor in lieu of the sofa. For being so thin, Abe can destroy a plate of danishes. I pluck another from the bag before they're all gone.

Abe goes to get dressed while Adam pulls out a street guide for me to go over our stops for the day. We're taking the tube to avoid traffic and parking. I want to see all the typical touristy sights—Big Ben, the London Eye, Buckingham Palace, the Globe, Westminster, and King's Cross.

Adam has been to London before and to all these places. I wonder if it bothers him as a photographer. Maybe he'd rather be out exploring new places than forced to babysit me.

"I could just go with Abe if that works better for you."

He looks up, his finger hovering over Cambridge. "What makes you say that?"

"You probably already have pictures of all these places. You probably don't want to see them again."

125

He scratches the side of his face, right by his ear. He hasn't shaved today, so he has a healthy day's worth of stubble on his face. It suits him, giving him a rough air.

"Sure, I've been here before, taken pictures of all these places at one time or another, but that doesn't mean any shots I take today won't be better. Besides"—he turns the map and points to a spot not far from where we'll be—"there is a small bridge here. The light was all wrong last time I was here. I want to stop there."

I stare at his finger. The light through the window catches a flake of icing still resting at the top. My mouth goes dry. He must notice it then too. I watch, transfixed, as he lifts his finger to his mouth and sucks. I gulp.

Needing to get away, I stand and walk into *our* room. We'll be leaving soon. I take my plastic box from my suitcase. I have a smaller container I can carry with me. It feels weird, carefully shaking some of her ashes into it.

I seal both containers tightly. I delicately tuck the bigger one back into my suitcase, and then I place the other in my purse. If I knew Adam wouldn't walk in, I would probably linger over them longer. Instead, I perch myself on the edge of my bed, facing the window.

It's a sunny day. The light streaming in illuminates tiny flicks of dust in its path. I have my cross-body bag slung over me and sitting in my lap.

"Ally," I whisper, "I'm in London on our trip. I have you with me. I'm not sure where I'm going to…put you yet. I want it to be somewhere beautiful." I pull the bag closer to myself. I can feel the outline of the box through the cloth material.

"I promise, somewhere beautiful."

"What were you saying?"

I jump, seeing Adam in the doorway. I didn't hear him open the door. I wipe away the moisture stinging the corner of my eye.

"Nothing. Are we heading out?" I stand, tucking a strand of hair behind my ear.

He nods and steps back, so I can move past him. Abe doesn't look ready. He's on the phone, pacing across the living room.

He holds up a finger and continues to pace, randomly saying, "Brilliant."

Adam and I watch him. Abe's long legs devour the small room. He turns and goes back to where he started. I'm about to sit down when he hangs up.

His eyes dance as he walks over to clap Adam on the shoulder. "Four tickets to the Arsenal match tomorrow."

Adam almost smiles. He looks over at me. "We're going to a football match tomorrow."

I'm confused. "Football?"

"You blokes call it soccer," Abe chimes in.

"Oh, cool."

Abe grins. "Very cool."

"Four tickets?" I adjust the strap of my purse, so it isn't rubbing my neck.

"My girlfriend, Shelly, is coming." He grabs his wallet off the kitchen counter and slips it into the back pocket of his jeans.

We take a cab to the station. It's silly, but I feel a thrill from thinking I'm underneath London right now. We're quiet for the ride.

Adam becomes Mr. Tour Guide once we're above ground. His camera hangs from his neck, half in and half out of its case. It's slightly overcast, but otherwise, it's nice out.

I feel like I've seen all of London by the time we stop for sandwiches. My feet are sore. I cross one leg over another and twist my foot at the ankle. We eat while sitting on benches near a park. Abe is trying to teach me cheers for the football match tomorrow.

Adam stands, crumbling his wrapper, and he tosses it into a nearby waste bin. "That place where I wanted to shoot is just down that path." He points. "I'll be twenty minutes."

After thirty minutes, I go after him. His back is to me as I walk up. My skin tingles as I take in the view before me.

We're near Cambridge. There's a small gray stone footbridge. It's rounded with two arched bends over the water that flows beneath it. A white swan idly paddles by in hopes of finding an errant crust of bread. A group of children play in a grassy area bordered with trees and flowers. It's a beautiful place.

It feels so right for Ally to be here. I can feel her presence so strongly. I blink away tears as I imagine her looking out over the water with the noise of playing children around her. She loved kids. It was why she worked in a daycare.

I lower myself and sit by a lonely tree on the edge of the park. I want to be discreet. With my hands, I push aside some of the mulch gathered at the base of the tree. I tap the container gently, releasing the ashes onto the soil and smooth the mulch back over the ashes before slipping the container back into my purse.

"I hope you're happy here, Ally. I feel you with me. It makes me think you like this place."

My hand lingers on the spot where a piece of her now rests. I lose myself in the moment—from the birdsong from the trees above me to the breeze that kisses my cheeks. This place smells old but in a good way, like worn leather and old books. It's not until he speaks that I remember I found this place because I was coming to look for Adam.

"What are you doing?" he asks, walking over to me.

I squint up at him. The sun has come out. "I came looking for you, and it is so pretty here that I thought I'd take a moment and enjoy it."

"Can I take your picture?"

I groan. "I'm not photogenic."

"I don't believe that," he argues.

My breath catches. I rest my hand back on the spot where Ally is, and I nod. He glances behind himself before taking a few steps back.

"Just look at the bridge, like you were doing before," he directs. "Now, close your eyes and tilt your head up. Now, down just a touch. Okay, right there."

I hear the click of his shutter and then nothing. I peek and see him now standing right above me, his hand out to help me up. I flex my hand against the earth one last time before brushing the dirt and mulch from my palms. Reaching up, I feel his hand wrap around mine before he pulls me up.

"Playing in the dirt?"

I nod. "You can't take me anywhere."

"What's taking you lot so long?"

We look up to see Abe approaching. His eyes widen when he sees my hand in Adam's. I tug my hand from his grasp and wipe it on the back of my jeans.

Adam bites back a smile. I look back at the tree.

"Coming?" Abe asks.

I turn and follow them back up the path.

There's a gift shop on the main road. I pop in to get something for my folks. I thought about buying a trinket, but instead, I get a postcard to send to my parents. When I'm at the register, I see a display of charm bracelets. On impulse, I grab one and a tiny Big Ben charm.

Adam and Abe are waiting for me just outside. I pull my bracelet out and attach the charm to it. I'm trying to hook it around my wrist when Adam takes it from me and does it for me.

I look up at him. "I could have…"

His head is bent, his long eyelashes lowered, as his eyes focus on my wrist. I drop my gaze to his hands. They are so big in comparison to the delicate clasp. Once the clasp is fastened, his fingertips dust my skin as he spins the bracelet around to look at the charm I bought.

"It's pretty," he says, dropping my hand.

My hand floats back down to my side before my brain catches up, and I remember I want to look at it as well. The chain is simple, silver with small links to attach the charms to. My Big Ben charm is silver as well, only the clockface is painted. It's forever three o'clock.

"Want to pop into a pub?" Abe asks. "I could use a drink."

My feet are still a bit sore, so I'm all for finding a place to sit for a bit longer. We don't have to walk long to find a place. It's bigger and less crowded than the place we were at last night.

I think back to Nigel and his offer to take me out while I am in town. I wonder if he could take my mind off of Adam.

The boys grab a table and let me buy this time. I carefully make my way over to the table with the drinks. Abe jumps up to grab their drinks, so I don't have to carry them the whole way.

"We should have just gone to a restaurant," Abe mumbles before taking a healthy swig of his ale.

"We didn't eat lunch that long ago." I laugh.

"Abe here is a growing boy," Adam says with mock seriousness.

I cover my mouth to muffle my laugh, trying to picture Abe any taller than he already is.

He glowers at Adam and turns his attention back to his drink. I drink my beer, the same Freedom Pilsner I had the day before. It's good, but I'll probably order water with dinner.

We only stay for one drink and then make our way to the London Eye. We eat somewhere near there before we go up, and then we'll head back to Abe's. After being unsuccessful in getting me to try some Scottish food, we end up at a Chinese place.

The line is long for the Eye. It works to our favor though as the skies darken, and Big Ben and Westminster Abbey are lit up. The ride is twenty minutes. I've never been crazy about heights. The capsule moves slowly enough that it doesn't bother me until we're close to the top. There are seats at either end. I sink into one and keep my eyes on the sights. It's fun seeing all the places we visited today from the sky. They seem somehow so small and big at the same time.

The ride back to Abe's flat is a quiet one. I think we're all exhausted.

I change in the bathroom. Adam is sitting on his bed, his laptop open in front of him when I return to the room. He must have changed for bed while I was in the bathroom. My eyes fail at avoiding his bare chest.

"I won't be long," he says, looking up. "I just wanted to upload the pictures I took today to my virtual hard drive."

"Thanks. Okay." I yawn. "Can I see them?"

He slides over, so there's a spot for me to sit next to him. Not much room. My arm presses against his, and I try to ignore the heat coming off of him. He waits for me to get settled and angles the laptop toward me before he starts the slide show. The slide show starts at the end of the day and goes backward. His pictures are beautiful. My chest swells when I see the pictures of me sitting under the tree. My eyes snap to his. He's waiting for my reaction.

"They're beautiful."

"Thanks," he says simply.

As the slide show continues, I feel my eyes growing heavy. It's been a long day, and while all his pictures are great, there are just so many, and there are so many of the same place but from different angles. I'm thinking I should probably move to my bed.

Then, I'm warm, maybe too warm, and my neck feels a bit stiff as I slowly wake up. It takes me a moment to figure out where I am, half sprawled across Adam. He's on his back, and I'm curled around him. My head is on his shoulder, my leg is hitched up on him, and my arm is draped across his chest. His very warm, very shirtless chest.

ELEVEN

I ease my leg off of him, freezing when I feel him stir beneath me. I wait a moment before lifting my arm from his chest, his beautiful chest. I pause, knowing I'll probably never be this close to it again. My eyes flick to his face to make sure he's still asleep before I do something I know I'm going to regret. I lick my lips and trail my fingertip across the ridge defining the cut of his pecs. My stomach flips.

I'm inching backward when I feel his arm tighten around me. I look up to see him gazing down at me with sleepy eyes, his hair falling into them.

"Don't I get a turn to touch you?"

My breath catches. I push his arm off me and sit up.

"I'm so sorry. I shouldn't have—"

He cuts me off with a shake of his head, reaching his hands to rest behind his head. "I didn't mind it."

I stand, needing some space between us, and I fiddle with the hem of my shirt.

"I'm going to go." I gesture to the door and hurry to the bathroom.

I'm sitting on the edge of the tub with my head in my hands when there's a knock at the door. "Yes," I say, lifting my head.

"You decent?" Adam asks through the door.

I jump up to check my reflection in the mirror, smoothing my hair behind my ears, before I open the door. I step backward as he charges in and closes the door behind him.

This is not a big bathroom. I feel short of breath while waiting for him to do or say something. My back is to the sink. He stands in front of me, resting his palms on the sink countertop behind me. This lowers his face so that we're eye level.

"I know you're attracted to me."

I gulp.

"Anything happening between us would be a bad idea," he continues.

My eyes narrow. "I never said I wanted anything to happen."

He straightens back up, his eyes moving to his reflection, and he pushes his hair off his face. He looks back down at me. "You didn't have to."

With that, he walks out of the bathroom, shutting the door behind him.

Asshole. What was that? I know you want me. What a jerk.

I take my shower even though I'll have to walk back to our room in my towel. I'm annoyed at him. I brush my teeth and finger comb my hair before I walk out.

The towel I'm using barely covers me. I hold on to it tightly as I pad across Abe's flat. Adam is getting something out of his bag when I walk in. I watch his eyes widen when he sees me.

"Could you…" I motion toward the open door.

He walks over to it, closes it, and leans his back against it, facing me. "Could I what, Aubrey?"

"Stop being weird and leave, so I can get dressed."

"Sure about that?" He smirks.

"Positive," I grit.

His mouth twitches before he turns and walks out into the living room. I lock the door behind him.

Our only plan for the day is the football match. After that, we're going to have dinner somewhere.

Once I'm dressed, I walk out to see Adam cooking breakfast. Abe is leaning on the counter while talking to him. I clear my throat, and they both look at me.

"I'm going to skip dinner tonight."

"Why?" Adam asks, turning his head back to the eggs he's scrambling.

"I'm going to call Nigel and see if he wants to go out."

Adam drops the spatula. "What?"

"I'm going to call—" I repeat slowly.

"I heard you," he snaps, picking the spatula back up. "Nope. I don't think it's a good idea."

I put my hand on my hip. "Are you trying to tell me I can't go?"

Abe is watching us like a spectator at a tennis match.

"That's exactly what I'm doing." Adam passes the spatula to Abe, who looks at it like it's a foreign object, before turning around to face me.

I shake my head. "You don't get to decide that. You are not the boss of me."

He crosses his arms over his still bare chest. "Why do you think I'm here, Aubrey? To watch out for you. Since I don't think you going out with some strange dude is a good idea, you are not going."

I step back into the room and grab my purse, pulling out my cell and Nigel's business card from it, and glare at Adam before I start dialing. "You don't get to decide this."

He marches over to me and plucks my phone out of my hand. He turns it off before he sets it on a tall cabinet next to us. He had to stretch to put it up there. Short of pulling a chair over or grabbing a step stool, I can't reach it.

"Give me back my phone," I huff.

He looks back at Abe. "Stir the eggs, man." Turning back to me, he leans down, so his face is in front of mine. "No."

I cross my arms over my chest. "I hope you know you are being ridiculous. I'm not a child. I don't understand why you think you can treat me like one."

He glares at me before glancing back to see that Abe is not stirring the eggs. Adam turns and makes his way back to the stove, putting his hand out for the spatula. He pushes the eggs around a couple of times before turning the heat off and moving the pan to a cool burner.

He turns back to me, using the spatula to gesture. A small bit of egg falls to the floor in front of him. Abe rolls his eyes and wipes it up with a takeaway napkin. Adam rubs his face with his other hand before tossing the spatula into the sink.

"I'm fine with you calling him but not with you going out alone with him."

My mouth drops. "That's not up to you."

He smirks. "I don't see what the issue is."

I lean against the bookshelf. "Give me my phone. Now."

He walks back over to me, standing right in front of me, and reaches up to grab my phone. He pauses, raising one eyebrow, before handing it to me.

I narrow my eyes at him. "I'm calling my father."

He seems to be holding back a grin. "You might want to check the time difference on your fancy watch first."

I glance down, tilting my wrist. I groan when I see it's the middle of the night at home. I push past him and storm into our room, shutting the door behind me. As the door clicks into place, I faintly hear Adam ask if I want any eggs.

This morning, I woke up in his arms, and yes, it's only because I fell asleep on him, but right now, I'd like to choke him. This is not how this trip was supposed to go.

I glance at the door as I lower myself onto the bed. I double-check the time, making sure it's not too early, and I call Nigel. He answers on the second ring and sounds happy to hear from me. He agrees to pick me up and take me out to dinner. I tell him where Abe lives and what time we should be back from the match. I'll just have to figure out a way to give Adam the slip.

There's a knock at the door, and I look up as Adam slowly opens it.

"Are you hungry?"

I nod, wishing I weren't, and stand. He steps back, so I can move past him. There's a plate that I think is for me on the countertop. I glance back at him to make sure, and he nods. I pick it up. I stay in the kitchen as he joins Abe in the living room.

They talk while they eat, so I finish first. I wash my plate and place it in the drying rack before going back into our room. I lie down, my back toward the door and face the window. It's more overcast today. I miss the light coming through the window.

When the door opens, I hold my breath. I can tell it's Adam. I don't think Abe would come in here.

"Are you going to pout all day?"

I flinch. "Are you going to keep bossing me around?"

He groans. "I'm not trying to boss you around. I'm trying to look out for you."

I turn over, facing him. "That's not how it feels."

He jams his hands into his pockets and slumps his shoulders, his head down. "Look, Aubrey, I'm responsible for you."

"I don't understand what the big deal is. Maybe if we were in a country where everyone didn't speak English, I'd understand."

He doesn't have a response to that.

We leave for the match once Shelly comes over. I like her right off the bat even though she talks a mile a minute, and I can barely understand her. Abe is so laid-back that they balance each other out. She's been visiting family in Ireland. Otherwise, we would have seen more of her.

She's the one who was able to get us the tickets to the match. Arsenal is playing Tottenham. I don't follow sports, especially ones happening in other countries, so Abe and Shelly try to fill me in on their rivalry on the way.

"Hopefully, Abe won't be too dashed if they lose. They aren't having the best year." She whispers.

Adam hears her and elbows Abe. "When did they win their last championship?"

Abe looks away and grumbles something that sounds like *eight years*. He changes the subject by trying to teach me some of their cheers.

Arsenal has some chants just for Tottenham. Nothing too clever, mainly, *Fuck Tottenham*. Abe looks embarrassed to cuss in front of me, and Shelly smacks him.

"I cuss. I totally cuss. You can cuss in front of me." I declare.

When they all start laughing at me, I glower.

"Whatever," I say, walking in front of them.

"No," Adam calls after me. "We want to hear you cuss."

Shelly runs to catch up with me and slips her arm through mine. "Ignore those rotten boys. I think you're lovely."

I smile at her and glance back at Adam to flip him off when we reach the car. Abe is driving, and

Shelly sits in the front passenger seat. Since Abe has to have his seat all the way back to accommodate his Lurch-like limbs, I'm practically in Adam's lap.

Being physically close to someone I am consciously trying to ignore is impossible. I'm hyperaware of Adam's every movement. If he moves, because of my perch, I feel it, and vice versa. Only, I don't think he's trying to ignore me. Or maybe he is because he isn't talking to me either.

We park blocks away from the stadium and walk. With their arms linked, Abe and Shelly walk in front of Adam and me. The sidewalk is tight, so while we walk, our arms brush.

I know I'm overreacting, but I'm still so upset. I logically can appreciate the fact that he's trying to look out for me, but I'm angry because he won't at least give me the benefit of the doubt to know when I need help.

Ally wanted me to find my independence on this trip. How am I supposed to do that if I need Adam's permission to do anything?

At the match, I sit next to Shelly, and Adam sits on the other side of Abe. I can feel him watching me as I chat with the couple next to me.

Is it going to be like this the whole trip? I might kill him before we leave Europe.

I stop thinking of him briefly when I get sucked into the excitement of the match. We're nearing the ninety-minute mark, and the score is one to one. The tension is palpable with each team wanting to score before the ref can extend the time.

There's a Tottenham corner kick that's particularly stressful. Abe holds his breath as Shelly clings to him. When the goalie clears it, half the stadium exhales. In the end, with an assist, an Arsenal striker is able to score, and the match ends. It's hard not to get caught up in the excitement at the win. We're hugging, laughing, and cheering.

I'm less annoyed at Adam. I'll have to wait and see how long that lasts.

When we get back to Abe's place, he and Adam run out to pick up some takeaway for us. As soon as they leave, I pounce on Shelly and tell her my plans to meet Nigel. She's a sweetheart and says she'll cover for me, but only after she programs her number into my phone and mine into hers. She makes me promise to call if I feel uncomfortable at any point.

I grab my purse and hurry to wait at the pizza place a block over. When I get there, I call Nigel, and he tells me he's on the way. Once I hang up, my phone starts ringing.

"Hello?"

"Where are you?" It's Adam, and he sounds pissed.

"I'm fine. You don't have to worry."

"Aubrey, get your ass back here right now."

I laugh. "You're crazy, you know that? I'm an adult. Please learn to accept it," I say before hanging up on him.

My phone starts ringing again. This time, it's Shelly.

"Hi, Shelly," I answer.

"Oh my God, Aubrey. Adam is pissed. Are you sure about this?"

I look up when I see Nigel walk in. "I'm positive. He's here. I have to go."

"Hey, Aubrey," he says, walking over to me.

"Hey, you." I grin.

"Ready?"

"As I'll ever be."

When we talked earlier, I asked a big favor from him.

He puts his arm around me as we walk to his car. "I made you an appointment if you still want to do it."

I nod. "Let's go."

My phone rings off and on the whole time we're out. I finally answer it when we're on the way back to Abe's flat.

"Hello?"

"Where are you?" Adam thunders.

I sigh. "I'm on the way back right now. Can you please relax?"

"I called your parents. They want you to call them."

Shit. "Way to overreact. Fine. I'll call them as soon as Nigel drops me off. Bye." I drop my phone into my purse and pinch the bridge of my nose.

"Everything okay?" Nigel asks sweetly.

I tilt my head, resting it against the headrest, and I smile at him. "I'm awesome. I can't thank you enough for taking me."

"It was a first for me too. Does it hurt?"

"I don't plan on touching it anytime soon."

He double-parks in front of Abe's flat. I unhook my belt and turn to thank him once more. His face is right there, and his lips find mine. I feel a bit dazed when he pulls back.

"Don't forget this." He passes me a paper bag from the pharmacy. "I have to say, this was enlightening."

He leans over to kiss me again. I jump at a sharp tap on my window. It's a hulking, glaring Adam.

"I better go. I'll email you," I say to Nigel.

"You better," he says. Only, his eyes are on Adam and not me.

I step out and am greeted with Adam losing it.

"You could have been killed."

I raise a brow at him and wave in the direction of Nigel's retreating car.

It's then that Adam sees the bandage peeking out from the neck of my shirt. "What happened? You were hurt."

146

His fingers are featherlight as they brush my hair to the side and ghost the edge of the bandage. I shrug away from his grasp and head up the stairs.

"Aubrey, wait. What happened to you?"

I turn and look down at him. "I got a tattoo. Happy? You acted like a lunatic and called my parents for nothing."

I turn and keep walking, hearing his footsteps behind me.

"You can't just take off like that. I'm responsible for you," he says from behind me.

I turn quickly and lean back when I realize how close he is behind me. "That's the whole issue. I'm calling my parents, so they can break it to you. I do not need a babysitter."

I pull my phone out of my purse and call them. After a few moments of assuring them that I am fine and I only went out with a new friend, I tell them to set Adam straight.

I pass him the phone and cringe when he says, "Did she mention she got a tattoo?"

My mouth drops as he hands the phone back to me.

"Hi."

It's my dad. "A tattoo?"

"Mmhmm. Are you mad?"

He laughs. "People don't get mad."

I finish for him. "Animals do. But for real, are you?"

There's a pause. "You are a grown woman, and we trust your judgment."

"Thank you. Can you please tell that to Adam?"

He agrees, and I pass the phone back to Adam. They talk for a minute, and he passes the phone back to me, so I can tell him I love them both and say good-bye.

"Was there anything you wanted to say to my dad?" I ask, offering my phone.

Our fingers brush as he takes it. He turns his face from my heated gaze.

"I'm sorry for any misunderstanding Sir." He offers quietly to my father.

It's not lost on me that he didn't offer me an apology. Adam follows me quietly the rest of the way up the stairs. Shelly and Abe must have heard us coming because they're waiting in the doorway.

"Oi! Let me see it right now." Shelly grins, pulling me into the flat.

I'm wearing a tank top under my T-shirt. It has a built-in bra, and I wore it on purpose. I slip my T-shirt off and ease my arm through the right strap of my tank. Shelly stands behind me, pulling the back of my top down to uncover the bandage. She gently peels it off to expose my tattoo. She pulls me to the bathroom, so I can look at it in the mirror at the same time. It's not big—maybe four inches across and six inches down.

"Did you lose someone?"

I didn't know Adam had followed us. He's leaning on the doorway. His gray eyes lock on mine. I nod and look at the pair of angel wings reflected in the mirror.

He takes the bandage from Shelly and delicately smooths it back on my shoulder. "I could have taken you."

I shake my head. "I was angry at you." I press the front of my tank top to my chest as I slip my arm back through the strap.

Adam holds the strap away from my shoulder, so it doesn't push against my bandage. Shelly looks back and forth between us before excusing herself. I turn around to face him. He picks up my hand and sets my phone in it.

"What did my dad say?"

He looks up at the ceiling. "It appears I have been a bit overly protective."

I touch his arm, and he looks down at me.

"I just don't want to feel smothered."

When he nods, I drop my hand.

"I saw him kiss you."

I gulp and take a step back, bumping into the sink.

"Do you like him?" He steps closer to me.

I lick my lips and watch his gray eyes flick to them. "I don't even know him."

"But you let him kiss you."

I can feel Adam's breath on my cheek. I blink. "I did."

"Did you like it?" He tucks a strand of hair behind my ear.

I feel all the tiny hairs on my earlobe stand straight up as the pad of his fingertip grazes it. My whole body is buzzing.

"I don't know."

His mouth twitches. "Why don't you know, Aubrey?"

I break our gaze. "I can't remember it."

He lifts his hand to my chin, tilting my face back to look at his. The pad of his thumb brushes across my lower lip. "Must not have been much of a kiss."

I'm frozen. I have no response.

I watch the tip of his tongue grace the edge of his bottom lip. My lips part when he drops his hand.

"You should always be able to remember a kiss," he says before walking out of the bathroom.

TWELVE

I stand there, leaning against the sink, and pant. It felt like Adam was going to kiss me. I thought he was going to kiss me. I wanted him to kiss me.

I still can't even remember Nigel's lips on mine. A pair of gray eyes erased them. I walk back into the living room, avoiding those eyes, as I pick up my T-shirt and put it back on.

"I'm going to go to bed."

"Oh, don't, love," Shelly calls out. "Please don't mind Adam. Come, and let's have a chat."

I glance over at Adam and Abe and hesitate.

She stands, grabbing my hand. She passes me a drink before grabbing one for herself. "We're going up to the roof." She holds her hand up when Abe moves to follow us. "No, my love. Girls only."

I'm relieved to be away from Adam, and I gratefully take a gulp from my beer once we're on the roof. "What's his problem?"

"Adam?" she guesses.

I nod before taking a healthy swig of my drink.

"He's a nice enough guy. I don't remember him being so tense the last time he was in town."

"He needs to chill out," I fume, still shaken by his intensity.

"He's usually the first to suggest a mad plan, YOLO and all that. I'm surprised he went mental over you going out."

I lean toward her. "What do you mean?"

With the exception of Abe and some other random friends they tweet-meet with, she's always considered Adam a loner. Sure, he'll meet up with people for a day here and there, but she was shocked when Abe said Adam would be going around the world with a girl.

"We totally assumed you guys were dating."

I shake my head too quickly and avoid her eyes after I see her brows rise. We end up staying on the roof for a couple of hours—gossiping about boys, school, parents, and not knowing what we want to be when we grow up.

Adam and I are leaving in the morning for Belgium. We'll spend a couple of nights there before we continue on to Paris. In three days, I will be in Paris.

I lock the bedroom door and get changed. I hurry to pull my shirt over my head when Adam knocks. I unlock the door and quickly slip into bed. Adam doesn't turn off the light, and he has his back to me when he pulls off his shirt. There, on his left shoulder, is his own tattoo—a cross wrapped in a pink ribbon.

I'm clambering out of my bed before I can stop myself. My fingertips trace the tattoo's outline. He stills under my touch.

"Who?"

I feel his back expand under my hand as he sucks in a deep breath. He turns, capturing my hands at the wrists and holding them between us.

"My mom."

"I'm so sorry," I rasp.

He lets go of my hands. "It was a long time ago."

My heart breaks. "How old were you?"

"Seven." He lifts his hand to the top of my bandage. "Who is this for?"

I close my eyes. "My aunt."

"When?"

I shake my head, feeling tears slip free. His thumbs brush them away, and he pulls me to him. My palms flatten on his chest as I press my face into his neck. His arms circle me, careful not to touch my bandage.

We stand like that for an eternity before I push off of him and back away in search of a tissue. There are some on a shelf by the window. I feel his eyes on me as I dry my tears.

"I'm sorry about that. I don't know what came over me."

"It's okay."

I turn and look at him, giving him a half smile, before I climb back into bed. I lie with my back to him.

The next morning, he's up and dressed before I awake. I'm greeted with fresh pastries when I walk out of our room. Adam must have walked to the bakery while I slept.

I take my shower and get changed before I eat. Abe isn't awake yet, but the train doesn't leave for a couple of hours.

When I sit, Adam turns on the microwave. When it dings, he pulls out a coffee mug and passes it to me.

"Thank you."

The silence is awkward between us. I secretly wish for Abe's or Shelly's presence to dilute the tension. The wait is not long.

Abe smells the pastries and comes out with Shelly trailing him in search of them. They're both still in their sleep clothes. I watch the affectionate way they cuddle and feed each other. I hug myself, enviously wanting to feel arms around me. Adam's arms.

"Did you change your bandage yet?"

I shake my head. Adam puts his hand out to help me stand.

"I'll help you."

We walk into the bedroom. I pull the pharmacy bag out and spread out the cream, gauze, and tape on top of the dresser. Adam steps out to wash his hands.

He closes the door behind him when he comes back in. The room instantly feels warmer. There's a mirror over the dresser. I watch him as he stands behind me. My shirt is loose. His eyes meet mine as he pulls it up and rests it over my shoulders. Goose bumps ripple across my skin when his thumb hits my skin right above my bra. I can't look away from him as he eases my right strap down.

He slowly peels the bandage from my skin. I flinch when he cleans my tattoo. He pauses, eyes never leaving mine, as he lowers his head and blows on it. My mouth drops open, and I grip the edge of the dresser. If it had not been right in front of me, I would have fallen over.

He lightly coats my tattoo in cream before he tapes a piece of gauze over it. Once he's done, he gently drags the strap of my bra back up my arm. I close my eyes and dip my head back as he lowers my shirt to cover my back.

My eyes flutter open when I hear the door open and close. I'm breathing heavily. I look at my flushed reflection in the mirror.

What just happened?

Neither of us speaks about it. Abe and Shelly take us to the train station. We say our good-byes and queue up for the train.

Once we're seated, I lose myself in a book. Adam is quiet, mainly looking out the window. It takes less than two hours to get to Bruges. We're staying in a small inn just outside the city. Thankfully, we have separate rooms with a connecting door. After this morning, I don't think I can sleep in the same room as him. We drop off our things and walk into the city.

"Hungry?"

I nod, sidestepping a man who stepped out into my path. Adam takes my arm, and my skin tingles underneath his fingers.

"Want a *gaufre?*"

It sounded like he said gopher. "Like the animal? No, not really."

He almost smiles. "It's French for waffle. It's one of three things you have to try in Belgium."

I knock my elbow lightly into his side. "Only three? What are the other two?"

He rubs his chin. He didn't shave this morning, and he is looking deliciously scruffy. "Normally, I'd say four things, but you don't like seafood, so for you, only three." He counts them off on his fingers. "Waffles, beer, and chocolate."

"What would the fourth be?"

He nods. "Mussels."

I make a face. "Yuck. Yeah, none of those for me."

He looks down at me. "No pressure, but if I order some and you decide randomly that you want to try a bite, just ask."

I purse my lips. Not going to happen.

We turn, and our surroundings suddenly feel older. We're in a courtyard. There are benches around a statue of two monks. They're standing, their bodies facing each other, but their heads are bent, foreheads resting on the other monk's shoulder. I circle it. It's simple—gray stone with lines so smooth. The vision is so sad. These monks are grieving together. I just don't know why.

I look up to see Adam lowering his camera.

"Do you know the story behind this?"

He shakes his head. I follow him along a path to another courtyard. The brickwork everywhere is beautiful. I've never seen anything like it. The detail so intricate, even in unexpected places like around windows and doorways.

There are canal boat tours and horse-drawn carriages. The clip-clop of the horses' hooves on the cobblestones makes me feel like I've stepped back in time.

We eat lunch on the patio of a restaurant across the square from where people queue up to take a carriage ride. There is a lovely bronze fountain with a horse head on each side where the horses drink.

As promised, Adam orders his mussels. They come out in a black cauldron-looking bowl with a lid. He flips the lid over to put the shells in.

He tilts his head. "Sure you don't want to try a bite?"

I shake my head, looking down at my gigantic serving of spaghetti. So, portion control is an issue here as well. Adam's meal comes with french fries, or *pommes frites*, as they call them here. They're delicious. He almost smiles when I steal some.

After lunch, the wind picks up. We're near the coast, and I'm cold. Adam shrugs off his sweater and gives it to me.

"But you'll be cold," I argue, already slipping it over my head.

As his scent surrounds me, I remember when it was his arms, not his shirt, wrapped around me. I try to take my mind off of him by popping into a shop.

I buy a piece of Belgian lace for my mom. The lace isn't heavy so I won't need to worry about the added weight to my bags. We pass a troubadour, a young girl playing the violin, as we explore. Adam puts some euros in her case.

We cross the canal and go to an area where there are warning signs to be quiet because women of God live there. It's behind a church. These women aren't nuns but simple holy women. The houses are like cottages, whitewashed with green shutters. There's a park area between the cottages and the church with paths and plaques that give information about the women who live here.

Every place I look becomes a potential site for Ally. I want the place I pick to make me feel the same way that the park in London made me feel.

As we walk, I watch Adam and the things he takes pictures of. He takes lots of extreme close-ups of simple things—doorknobs, hinges, iron rings, and fastenings.

We spend the rest of the day like that, exploring.

By the time we make it back to the inn, I'm exhausted. Adam runs out to get us dinner. He promises he'll get something simple.

The bags he returns with smell delicious.

"God, that smells good," I sigh when he walks into my room. "What did you get?"

"Ever had a *croque-monsieur?*" he asks.

"In English?"

He almost smiles as he passes me something wrapped in deli paper. "A grilled ham and cheese."

"Yum. Thank you so much," I say, tearing open the wrapping.

He also got us some bottled water. "Tomorrow, Belgian beer," he says solemnly.

I shake my head at him and inhale my sandwich. After we eat, he goes to his room, closing the door between us, so I can change for bed. I'm settling under the covers when I hear a light tap on the door.

"Come in."

Adam slowly opens the door, pausing when he sees I'm in bed. "Your tattoo. You probably need to…"

"Oh," I groan, sitting up. "I completely forgot." I start to push off the covers.

"Stay there. Where's the bag that had everything in it?"

I point to the dresser on the other side of the room. He gets it, and then he comes and sits next to me. I scoot over to give him more room. I slip my arm out of the sleeve of my T-shirt, holding the front of it tight to my chest. Cool air hits my back, making me shiver. He carefully pulls off my old dressing. It doesn't sting much this time when he cleans it.

His fingertips stroke my shoulder as he covers it with cream. Unwelcome desire blooms within my gut. Thank God he can't see my face. I'm sure I must be flushed. I cringe, wondering if my neck is red too. I try to think of anything else. I start wondering about what my parents are doing right now.

Before I know it, I'm nodding off. A combination of his gentle touch and all the walking we did today sends me over the edge. I don't remember falling asleep.

The next morning, I wake up, bandaged and with my arm back inside my shirt. I'm not certain how either of this happened, and I'm not asking.

We take the train to get near Bouillon in the Ardennes. At the train station, Adam rents a car to drive us the rest of the way. We take a long, winding two-lane road most of the way. It's mainly farmland with wide expanses of green dotted with cows and clusters of modern-looking windmills.

Adam is quiet. It's not that he talks a lot in general, but the silence feels strange. We've been together for five days now. I thought it would be easier by now.

We're staying in the summer cottage belonging to the parents of one of Adam's photographer friends. The driveway is hidden from the main road. We pass it twice before we find it. It's small but quaint. The cottage has been visited off and on all summer, so there's at least enough food to throw lunch together. Adam makes caprese salad that we eat with bread.

After lunch, we head into town. We visit the Castle Bouillon. It sits high on a hill with the Semois River curving around it. Adam is still inside taking pictures when I walk outside. From the entrance to the right, there's a path I take.

This is where I meet Godfrey of Bouillon or his statue. He's an opposing figure, carrying his signals. Not far from him is a shade tree.

I know, looking around, that this is where Ally would want to be. I sit next to the tree, like I did in London, only there is no mulch around this tree. I push some dirt aside, near the base of the tree. I look around quickly for Adam or anyone else. I'm not sure if scattering ashes is allowed here, so I empty the container quickly and slip it back in my purse.

I smooth dirt over her ashes and close my eyes. When I open them, I see Adam walking toward me. I stand, brushing the dirt off my hands.

"Want to go to a Belgian wedding?" He's tilting his head to a group of people waving at me from behind him.

I laugh, giving them a half wave. "Whose wedding?"

He points out an older gentleman. "That's the father of the groom."

I look down at my jeans and T-shirt. "We aren't dressed for a wedding."

He shrugs. "Did you pack a dress? We can run back and change."

I shake my head as I agree, and then I follow Adam up the hill. I assume he's finding out where and when we need to meet them as I stand awkwardly next to him.

I've heard him speak French since we've been here but only one-off sentences, not full-on conversations. Another thing I did not know about Adam, he's clearly fluent in French. I blink when I realize he's staring at me.

"Ready?" he asks.

I nod, and we make our way back to the car. He pulls into the driveway on the first try.

Since we have almost no time to get ready, I skip taking another shower and change into a simple boatneck-style print dress. It's still overcast. I frown while slipping on my sandals, knowing my feet will be cold, but they're the only shoes I packed that match the dress.

Adam is telling me to hurry as I do my hair and makeup as fast as I can. If I had more time, I'd curl my hair, but instead, I sweep it to the side with a simple silver clip. Adam knocks on my door as I dig in my backpack for my black scarf, thinking I can use it as a wrap.

"Come in."

I hear the door creak open.

"We need to get…" He pauses. "That dress is short."

I glance back at him. He knows how to wear a suit.

I cringe, turning around. "Is it too short?"

I have a hard time buying dresses because I have a long torso. This dress hits only a couple of inches above my knee. I tug at the hem in an effort

163

to lengthen it while I wait for him to answer. His eyes start at my feet before drifting slowly up my body. When they finally rest on my face, I gulp.

He scratches the back of his head. "I guess it's okay," he says before turning and walking out of my room. "Let's go," he says from the hallway.

"Just okay," I grumble, turning back to finish looking for my wrap.

Once I have it, I put some euros and my passport into my clutch, and I hurry after Adam. He's leaning against the wall by the front door. When he sees me, he straightens and opens the front door for me. I slip past him, forcing myself not to linger and breathe in his cologne.

It's a short drive to the government center. In the car, Adam explains that in Belgium, you have to be legally married before the church ceremony.

When we get there, I feel self-conscious. I know we were invited, but it still feels like we're crashing.

The legal ceremony is standing-room only. A woman with a sash, not unlike Miss America, says a whole bunch of stuff I don't understand before having the bride and groom sign something. After that, everyone claps, and we all walk a block to the church.

The ceremony seems similar to weddings I've been to in the States. There's a bit of a laugh when a young boy who's part of the wedding party steps on the bride's veil. Her head jerks back, and I'm amazed the veil doesn't rip.

From the church, we follow them to a chateau for the dinner and reception. It's a beautiful stone building with dark wood floors and a large courtyard. I'm happy to stay inside where it's warm, but the sun comes out.

"Come, come. *Il faut qu'on aille au jardin*," the father of the bride says, pulling us toward the courtyard.

"Why are we going outside? It's cold," I ask Adam.

"You must taste the Belgian sun," the father of the bride answers for Adam.

Adam raises his eyebrows and puts his elbow out for me to take. "Can't not taste the Belgian sun, Aubrey."

I'm from California. It's less of a big deal to me when the sun comes out. Even though it's much more comfortable inside, everyone is outside, enjoying the sunshine—except for me. I'm freezing my ass off.

When my teeth start to chatter, Adam decides we've tasted enough sun, and he takes me back inside. He stays with me, but I can tell by the way he absentmindedly strokes his camera that he'd rather be outside, taking pictures.

"Go."

His eyes snap to mine.

I give him a halfhearted push toward the door. "I'll be fine. I'll get a drink. How do I order a beer?"

"I'll get you one first." He turns to the bar.

"Adam, I can get my own beer. Now, go outside and eat some sun."

He almost smiles.

I make my way to the bar and manage to order my own drink. I wander around the main floor. There's a large dining room with an area for dancing by the DJ.

I'm looking for the restroom when people start filing back inside. I've just found it when I catch a glimpse of Adam.

I can't figure him out. Back in New York, those things he said about me, when he thought I couldn't hear him. He seemed like a jerk. Then, in London, he was so bossy. After he spoke with my dad, he seemed to relax, but I can tell he wants to hover.

As random last-minute guests, our table is far from the wedding party. It turns out two guests fell ill and were unable to make it. That's the only reason we're here.

The meal is served in multiple courses—the first being soup followed by a salad and a salmon plate. Great. I eat the salad, except for the chunks of blue cheese. Adam watches me eat, but thankfully, he doesn't say a word. The next course is a filet mignon with potatoes and asparagus. The filet is melt-on-your-tongue good.

During the meal, toasts are made from the attendants and then the parents of the bride and groom. It's all in French, so Adam leans into me, his hushed breath on my ear, as he translates for me. I shiver and pick at my nail polish, hoping he doesn't notice.

A sorbet is served next to cleanse our palates before the cake. Before the cake is served, the DJ changes the ambient background music to dance music. The tables empty as guests get up to dance.

Is Adam going to ask me to dance with him? Before he can, a tall dark-haired young man with an impish grin does. I start to shake my head, but that doesn't seem to be an acceptable response. The man grasps my hand and pulls me to the dance floor anyway. I shoot a panicked look to Adam, who just shrugs.

At least the music is familiar, all American Top 40 hits. I haven't been dancing in forever. I'm awkward, especially in the arms of a man whom I can't understand. When the song ends, I go to make my escape, only to end up in the grasp of another man.

He's not as tall as the man I danced with before, and he speaks broken English. His name is Cedric. To speak over the music, he brings his face really close to mine. I give him a confused look when he asks if I can rap.

"Like sing?" I ask.

He bobs his head up and down, smiling widely.

I shake my head. "No, I can't rap."

He looks so disappointed that I almost feel bad.

Then, he asks if Adam is my boyfriend. I glance back to where Adam is sitting. A stunning brunette woman is now occupying my seat. Adam's eyes flash to mine before I quickly turn my head back to Cedric.

"No, he isn't."

When the song ends, I start to leave the dance floor in search of water when an arm circles my waist. I start to turn to decline whoever it is, and I freeze when I see it's Adam. I should have known. A moment's reflection is all it takes to recognize his scent around me. My eyes flick to his hand. His palm is flat against my stomach with my back to his chest.

He lifts one of my hands and wraps it around his neck, pulling me closer to him. I lean back on him, my hips matching the sway of his. His breath is hot on my neck as his other hand drifts down my side to grip my hip. Instinctively, my fingers thread their way into his hair and tug.

"Careful," he growls in my ear.

I ignore him and rest my head on his shoulder as his hips grind against me. I'm not sure if I've ever been this turned-on. There is something about him, even when I feel like kicking him, that pulls me to him.

The song ends before I'm ready for it to. I start to pull away, more for the sake of pride than anything else. His grip briefly tightens around my waist before he lets me go.

"I need water," I explain, turning to face him, my fingers gesturing toward my throat in case he couldn't hear me over the music.

He nods and walks with me, his hand scorching me through the thin material of my dress as he rests it on the small of my back. He orders for me and gets a beer for himself. Then, he laughs when I drain my water and ask for another.

"We leave tomorrow. You haven't had a Belgian beer yet."

I shake my head. "I had one earlier when I got cold and came inside."

"So?" He tilts his head.

I shrug. "It was good. I'm just more of a water girl. I haven't been dancing in..." I trail off.

"Come on, you're young. I bet you're out partying every weekend."

I shrug. It doesn't seem like he'll believe me either way.

We find the bride and groom to congratulate them, and then we thank the bride's father for inviting us before we leave. We could have stayed longer, but the plan is to drive to Paris in the morning.

I've just changed out of my dress when Adam knocks on my door.

"Yes?" I ask, opening the door.

He holds up a bar of chocolate with an elephant on a red wrapper. "Belgian chocolate time."

I follow him out to the living room and sit next to him on the sofa, tucking my legs under me. He breaks a piece off for each of us and passes one to me.

"*Côte-d'Or*," I say out loud, reading it off of the piece.

"My favorite," he replies solemnly.

"There's an elephant on it." I look back at him. "How is that Belgian?"

He slowly chews his piece before answering me. "I think the cocoa comes from Africa."

I take a bite and let it melt on my tongue. My eyes close, and my head falls back as the most perfect piece of chocolate crashes my senses like a tidal wave. It's smooth and rich without being overly sweet.

"You look like you might need a private moment," Adam jokes.

I stare at the piece still in my hand and look back at him. "This is the best piece of chocolate I've ever had."

He almost smiles before popping another piece into his mouth.

THIRTEEN

I sleep most of the way to Paris. I awake to Adam shaking my shoulder. I blink my eyes open and glance around. We're in a parking garage. When I don't immediately move to get out of the car, Adam shakes my shoulder again.

"Mmmkay," I grumble, getting out.

"It's Paris. Aren't you excited?"

I raise one arm above my head and stretch. "There's only so much excitement I can muster within five minutes of waking up."

He opens the trunk and pulls out his camera case. "Should we go to a café first?"

I have always wanted to sit at a sidewalk café in Paris with a coffee and some french bread. I grin as I nod, already feeling more awake.

As we walk out of the underground parking lot, my jaw drops. In front of us is the Arc de Triomphe. I can see people standing around and underneath it, but it's in the center of a busy roundabout.

"How do we get over there?" I ask, eyeing the traffic.

He laughs and points to what looks like an underground subway entrance. "No need to run across the street. There's a tunnel."

"What's that line for?" I ask, looking at the swell of people queued up for something.

"To stand on top."

My mouth drops. "No way! I didn't know you could do that."

Our flight to Africa leaves in the morning. We decided ahead of time that we would skip some things if the lines were long.

I pout and look back at the line. I didn't know you could stand on top of the Arc de Triomphe.

When we exit the tunnel, we are right under it. From up close, the stonework is amazing.

"What are all the names for?" I ask, tilting my head and shading my eyes from the sun.

"To commemorate those who fought in a battle."

I'm not hip on French history. "Which one?"

He pauses his camera raised just halfway to his face before he shrugs. "Not sure."

I laugh and follow him as he takes shot after shot. I pull out my phone and take a couple for myself.

"Did you want to go up top?"

I shake my head. "The line is too long. Since we parked near here, can we check it out again before we head to the hotel?"

"Sure."

We go back into the tunnel and take the underground pathway to the other side of the street, away from where we came, and we sit down at a sidewalk café.

"Once the food is out, will you take my picture?"

Adam nods as he glances at the menu. The tables are tiny and set stadium-style, facing the sidewalk. After he reads the menu to me, I tell him what I'd like, and he orders.

Once our food comes, he has to push our table forward and slide past me to take my picture. I feel very Parisian once I put my sunglasses on and sip my coffee for the picture.

As appealing as it would be, we don't linger. There are too many things to see. We have tickets for a double-decker red tour bus that we can hop on and off of at each of its stops. When we're ready to go to the next stop, we just board any available bus in its fleet.

When we board, we're given earbuds, so we can listen to an audio tour between each stop. Adam smirks at me when I offer to plug his in. Our first stop is the Paris Opera house. As pretty as it is, we decide to stay on the bus until the Eiffel Tower.

"What? Too good for the audio tour?" I tease.

He rolls his eyes, crossing his arms. "Not my first go-around on the big red bus."

Part of me feels bad that he's stuck with me, going to places he's already seen. I know he's excited about Africa. He's never been to Victoria Falls or on a safari.

We exit the bus at the Eiffel Tower. The line is awful, but this is one thing I am willing to wait for. There are gardens across the street that Adam explores while I hold our place in line. He isn't gone long and seems happy with some of the pictures he was able to take of people sunbathing and strolling through the greenery. He clicks through them, holding his camera up, so I can see a few.

We buy tickets and take the stairs to the first level. At first, I argue that I want to take the lift, but Adam has done it before, and once I see the line difference, it makes sense.

Standing there, holding on to the railing of the Eiffel Tower, is surreal, like something out of a movie. I glance back at Adam. He's taking a picture of the bottom of the lift as it moves upward toward the next level. I've noticed he likes taking pictures of things more than people.

He focuses his lens on the intersection of two pieces of metal. Behind him, I can see a couple kissing. I turn to look around and see two more couples embracing. I'm in the most romantic city in the world with a gorgeous man who doesn't seem interested in me at all.

I turn my back to him and walk away. I try to picture Ally here. Would she have taken her trip alone or gone with a boyfriend? I remember her always having a date for family barbeques. Would she be here right now, being kissed, if she had gotten better?

I jump when someone taps me on my shoulder, and I turn to see a handsome blond man with his arm around a petite brunette woman.

He holds his camera out toward me in the universally translatable gesture of, *Will you take our picture?*

They don't speak English. If I had to guess, I think they're speaking Russian. I have them lined up in the viewfinder when the camera is plucked out of my hands.

"Hey!"

Adam shrugs and takes a few pictures of them from different angles rather than my boring straight-on stance. I'm annoyed. It was rude of him to just take the camera from me. As Adam returns the camera to the blond man, the look of sympathy in my direction from the petite woman embarrasses me.

Adam picks up on my mood change. "What's wrong?"

I lie, "I'm just ready to go to the next place."

"You sure?"

I nod, looking everywhere but in his eyes.

Once we're back on the bus, I put my earbuds back in. I'm being immature, and I know it. I should just tell him what he did to upset me. Instead, I give him the silent treatment. What's worse is he can tell I'm annoyed, and he is now acting defensive and irked.

I had this vision of Paris in my mind, maybe from movies or novels. Reality is not living up to the fantasy.

Our next stop is the Louvre. Travel guides make it clear that you could spend days alone looking at all the artwork held there. Since we only have this one day in Paris, our plan is to go into the courtyard to see the glass pyramid and underground to see the rest of the pyramid.

It's crowded with people going in every direction. The closer we get to the line to go inside, the greater the feeling of awe I feel in my chest, knowing that the original works of the most famous artists reside within these walls. I'm having an emotional reaction to being near such greatness even though I'm not going to see them. Just knowing they're there is enough. When Adam isn't looking, I reach down, pick up a stone, and slip it into my pocket.

We take some pictures and leave quickly. The crowds are overwhelming, and once the feeling of being near great art wears off, a feeling of claustrophobia sets in.

We cross the street, and since a bus isn't there for us to board, Adam leads me to a nearby bridge. The Louvre sits along the Seine. The bridge closest to it appears almost golden in the morning light. As we get closer, I can see that it isn't the bridge but the brass padlocks covering its sides that are golden.

I trail my fingers across one. There's a date written on it in green marker. I've heard of these. I think I read a book that talked about them.

Adam pulls out his camera to take a picture of a couple farther down the bridge as they attach a lock to it, and then they throw the key into the river. The lock symbolizes their union, their commitment to each other. It's romantic, again reminding me of where I am and who I'm with.

I take a few pictures of my own before we walk back to catch the bus. By the end of the day, we have seen the major attractions of Paris. I'm exhausted and still feeling sorry for myself, even with Adam by my side I am alone in a crowded city. I miss Ally.

Our hotel is between the airport and Montmartre. We check in before driving closer to Montmartre to walk around and have dinner.

It's strange how we spent a good portion of the day sitting on the bus, but I'm still exhausted. Adam doesn't seem as affected as I am. I wonder if he thinks I'm a dull companion.

"Was Paris everything you imagined?" he asks over dinner.

I think back to the couples we saw on the Eiffel Tower and on the bridge by the Louvre. "Seemed to be more of a city for couples."

He tilts his head and looks at me. "You're probably right."

I doze off on the way back to the hotel.

I wake up to Adam shifting me in his arms as he attempts to open the door to my room. I turn my face into his neck and inhale, filling my senses with his musk. If I were more awake, I would tell him to put me down, that I could walk. I don't. I enjoy the feel of his arms around me.

As he lowers me to my bed, I coil my arms around his neck and whisper, "Stay with me," in his ear.

He jerks his head back and looks at me with wide eyes. "What are you saying?"

I groan, "Ugh. Never mind. I just thought you were comfy."

He moves toward me, but I shake my head. The way he reacted embarrasses me, and now, I just want him gone.

Our rooms are separated by an interior door. He hesitates, looking back at me, before going into his room. I sit up and hurry across the room to lock my side of the door before collapsing back into bed and allowing my exhaustion to overtake me.

His angry banging on the interior door is what awakes me the next morning.

"What?" I yell, half awake, stumbling to the door.

"Why did you lock the door? It's time to wake up," he snaps through the door.

"I'm awake, and I locked the door because I wanted to," I huff.

There's a pause. I turn to make my way to the bathroom when I hear him grumble, "You're acting like a child, Aubrey."

My mouth drops open, and I storm back toward the door, unlocking it before I fling it open.

"Locking a door makes me a child?" I fume, charging him.

He shrugs. "Just because I didn't want to sleep with you—"

I cut him off. "Sleep with me?"

He crosses his arms. "Yeah, 'cause I'm so comfy."

I blush, wishing I could disappear right then. "Trust me, I won't make that mistake again."

I slam the door in his face.

"We need to leave in thirty minutes," he orders through the door.

I contemplate ways of murdering him as I crouch under the too short ancient showerhead. I could push him in front of one of those big red buses, maybe drop-kick him into the Seine. After he suffers no fewer than ten deaths by my hand,

I'm in a much better mood, and I beat him to the lobby.

His hair looks strange. I have to stifle a laugh as I picture him trying to fit under his showerhead. Maybe he wasn't able to wash out all of his shampoo.

Our flight from Paris to Zambia has a layover in South Africa. It doesn't really make sense to me that we're flying past Zambia and will then backtrack. The Livingstone Airport is not as big as the O.R. Tambo Airport. It's a ten-hour flight there, then a four-hour layover, followed by another two-hour flight to get to Zambia.

Originally, I wanted to go see the pyramids, but my dad was nervous about the recent political unrest in the country, and he wanted me to avoid it. I can't argue with his logic.

While we were planning this trip, when Adam originally suggested a stop at Victoria Falls, I had to Google it to know for sure where it is. It rests on the borders of Zambia and Zimbabwe with national parks on both sides.

We're staying on the Zambia side at the Royal Chundu. The accommodations are on the expensive side, but the added security was important to my mom and dad.

A shuttle takes us from the airport straight to the lodge. The pictures online do not do it justice. All milk chocolate wood with crisp white accents. We're sharing a suite, our rooms separated by a lounge.

I trail my fingers across the mosquito netting draped over my king-sized bed. It's both romantic and a reminder of the dangers that exist, even in paradise. I open the door to the balcony off my room. We're on the second floor, overlooking a pool.

"You're lucky we're in a hotel."

I look up to see Adam leaning against my doorway. "How come?"

"It's considered rude not to eat what you are served in Zambian households."

I pause. "What do they usually serve?"

He almost smiles. "Grasshoppers are considered a delicacy in some parts of Zambia."

I wrinkle my nose. That does not sound appetizing. "That can't be all they eat," I argue.

He pushes off the doorframe and crosses my room, walking in front of me. Moving the sheer fabric of the curtain aside, he looks out the window before looking back at me.

"This close to the Zambezi River?" He makes it a question that he answers for me. "The most common dish is freshwater fish."

I shiver. "Do you think that's all they serve here?"

181

He reads my panicked expression and has had his fun. "I'm sure they'll have something simple that you'll like."

I nod hesitantly, not really believing him. We have both had a long day. I'm a bit hungry but sleep has the greater siren call. He reminds me to make sure my net is secure before retreating to his side of the suite.

I wonder what he thinks of me. I cringe, remembering the night before when I asked him to stay with me.

One part of traveling that is not growing on me is the sensation of waking up in a different bed every night. It seems adventurous in your head, but the actuality of those first few moments of waking before you remember where you are can be unsettling.

I shower, knowing we'll have our breakfast in the main dining room of the lodge. I want to make a good impression. I pad barefoot across the suite to check on Adam. I'm nervous about the idea of venturing off on my own, and I hope he's up and ready for breakfast as well.

His door is cracked. I gently push it open wider to peer inside. Other than that morning in London when he caught me watching him sleep, he usually wakes up before me.

The netting leaves little privacy to hide his shirtless frame from me. I'm mesmerized by the gentle rise and fall of his chest as he sleeps peacefully. Not wanting to be caught and not able to put off breakfast, I quietly pull his door back to its original cracked stance.

I pad back to my room to slip on tennis shoes, and making sure I have a key card in my back pocket, I leave our room in search of food. The lodge is inclusive, so food and drinks are covered during our stay.

We passed the dining room when we checked in last night, so it's easy for me to find. I'm quickly seated and provided a menu that is thankfully in English. I order nshima, a simple sugared porridge with fruit on the side to go with my coffee.

There's an Australian family seated at the table next to me. When they see I'm alone, they convince our server to push our tables together, so I won't have to eat alone. I try to stop them, to tell them I'm fine. It's embarrassing the way the other diners stare as our tables are combined. I'm annoyed at their pushy friendliness until their son joins our table. Then, I'm quite grateful for their insistence.

His name is Conner. He's tall and fit in the way that if he lived in the States, I would assume he was a football quarterback. He's twenty-five and easy to talk to. He explains this grand trip is an annual thing his folks have done ever since he was ten years old. This is their third time back to Victoria Falls. He pauses and looks behind me.

"Why didn't you wake me up?"

I turn to see Adam glaring at me. "You looked comfortable, Adam."

I turn back toward Conner and his family to introduce them. Adam continues to fume while a waiter sets a place for him next to me.

After he sits, I whisper, "Why are you acting so annoyed?"

He ignores me, so I turn back to Conner and pick up where we left off. Conner's mom is able to get Adam to stop pouting and talk. I already told them about our trip so far and where we're headed. They're curious, or at least seem to be, about his previous trips. While they speak, Conner asks if I'd like a tour of the grounds around the lodge. Adam's head snaps in my direction when he hears me accept, and I excuse myself from the table.

His hand rises to gently wrap around my wrist, stopping me. "Where are you going?"

I stare down at his hand, his fingers hot against my skin. "Conner and his family have been here before. He offered to show me around."

He looks up at Conner, who seems equally interested in Adam's grip on my wrist, before he opens his grasp, freeing me. Conner directs me to a side exit, his hand drifting to the small of my back. I turn to look over my shoulder before we pass through the door, and I lock eyes briefly with Adam. His eyes are hard as they hold mine until I pass through the doorway.

"Are you two dating?"

My attention flies back to Conner. When we were sitting, his height wasn't as apparent. I have to crane my neck to look up at him.

"Adam?" I ask, even though I knew that's who he meant.

"I don't mean to pry. He just seems…" He pauses. "Possessive."

I fold my arms across my chest. "He thinks he's my babysitter," I grumble.

Conner blinks. "I'm sorry. That wasn't the impression I got from him."

I shake my head. "Trust me, he just enjoys bossing me around. I had to ditch him in London to go have fun."

He directs me over to a bench by one of the pristine swimming pools. "This I have to hear."

I sit next to him, our legs touching, and I grin. "I got a tattoo."

"Brilliant." He laughs. "What did you get? Can I see it?"

I turn, so my back is to him, and I pull at the neck of my shirt. "I'm not sure if you can see it."

He peers down the back of my shirt. "Is it a bird?"

"They're angel wings," I whisper, thinking of Ally as I look back at him.

The wind has picked up, and he tucks a strand of hair that is dancing wildly across my face behind my ear.

"We'll have to come up with something, so you can ditch him here as well."

I raise my brows. "What do you propose?"

FOURTEEN

Once our plan is settled, Conner walks me back to my room.

Adam is waiting, sitting on the sofa in the lounge. "Our tour to the falls leaves in thirty minutes," he reminds me gruffly.

"Geez, did you wake up on the wrong side of the bed or what?" I snap.

He moves his computer from his lap to the coffee table in front of him. "Excuse me?"

I shake my head. "Seriously, you were so rude at breakfast, and now, you're all pissy here, too. Are you annoyed at me for something?"

He stands, rubbing his face, as he walks over to me. "As much as it annoys you, I'm supposed to be looking out for you. When I wake up and you're not here and there's no note or anything explaining where you went, I get annoyed."

My mouth drops. "You, for real, want me to wake you up before I go eat?"

He rolls his eyes, and I restrain the desire to stomp on his foot.

"You could have left a note."

As annoying as he is, he does have a point there. I guess.

"Well, what about when you saw that I was fine in the dining hall? Why were you still annoyed then and now?"

He rubs both of his temples as though I'm causing him mental pain. "You just go off with random strangers. Do you get how dangerous that can be?"

I move past him toward my room. "Do you think I'm an idiot? Conner is there with his family. Do you think he would do something to me after his mother watched us walk away together?"

"What about Nigel?"

I turn and glare at him. "Nigel didn't do anything to me."

"He kissed you."

"This conversation is ridiculous. I'm done explaining myself to you!" I shout, slamming the door in his face.

My heart is pounding as anger and annoyance seep from my pores. I storm around my room, throwing things in my cross-body bag. The moment my hand touches Ally's ashes, I sink to the floor and cry, cradling the box in my arms. This trip isn't about Adam or how much he annoys me. It's about Ally and doing what she wasn't able to do.

I feel silly and childish. I need to focus on what's important instead of letting him get under my skin.

Now calm, anger banished, I carefully pack the smaller box with some of her ashes into my bag. Adam is waiting for me by the door. I don't ignore him. I just nod in his direction as I move past him. That's all the maturity I am able to currently summon.

We are part of a group tour leaving from the lodge to the falls. A British explorer named the falls after Queen Victoria, but the locals still call them Mosi-oa-Tunya, which means smoke that thunders, and thunder it does. I've seen smaller waterfalls, but nothing could have prepared me for the roar of the falls as our van approaches them.

I sit next to Conner. We speak until it becomes impossible. I slip my waterproof windbreaker out of my bag and put it on before we get out of the van. There are only ten of us in this group.

Adam's annoyance with me seems forgotten as he focuses on capturing as many images as he can. The falls are not the tallest or the widest in the world. Our guide explains though that its combined height and width make it the largest waterfall in the world. Islands dotting the river are close to the falls, so we can explore them with a different tour offered by the lodge if we want to.

Depending on the time of year, there's even a section of the falls that form a natural stone lip where people can swim since the threat of going over is smaller. It's called the Devil's Pool. As exciting as looking out over the edge of a waterfall would be, I just couldn't picture myself actually doing it. While not deathly afraid of heights, I'm not a fan of them either.

I spend most of our tour with Conner. It seems almost funny how annoyed Adam was, considering how uninterested in my whereabouts he currently is.

Talking near the falls is impossible over their roar. We're on the side facing them when I get distracted and start to stumble. A hand reaches out to stop my fall. I assume it's Conner, and I blush when I realize it's Adam who steadies me. Maybe he isn't as uninterested as I thought.

He charges ahead and away from me while I form the words to thank him. He's already too far away to hear them. Conner isn't far from us and sees what happened. When his eyebrows rise, I shrug. There really is no explaining Adam.

We stop for a picnic-style lunch, provided by the lodge, next to the falls. The main dish is fish. I fill my plate with cheese, bread, and fruit instead. There's something that looks like beef jerky, but thinking it looks spicy, I avoid that as well.

Adam sits on one side of me, and Conner is on the other. I glance at Conner before I yawn and admit a nap would be nice once we're back at Royal Chundu. I peek at Adam, hoping he believes me.

After our plates are cleared, I make my way closer to the best view of the falls, and I sit down on a large gray rock. A fine mist of spray reaches my face. I glance around me before slipping the container of Ally's ashes from my bag.

This waterfall represents so many things Ally loved—nature, the idea of feeling so small in such a big world, and the flow of life. The water moves across its course. It does not hesitate as it breaches the unknown and flows freely to the pool below. Making sure her ashes don't get caught in the breeze, I tap them out onto the ground in front of the rock I'm sitting on.

I don't cover them with earth as I did in England and Belgium. I'm comforted by the thought of the mist of the mighty falls reaching her. She would have loved to feel it if she were here, but this is as good as I can do.

I slip the container back into my bag and lean back on my palms to take in the overwhelming magnificence of the sight before me. Only this time, I feel her with me. I watch the flight of a small bird cross over the rushing water to land in the trees of one of the islands hugging the edge of the falls.

A tap on my shoulder breaks the spell I'm under. It's Conner. I follow the direction of his hand as he points to the van that brought us here. I watch as Adam climbs into it before I stand and walk over with Conner.

Adam is sitting in the back row, his face focused downward, as he scrolls through the pictures he took. When we get back to the lodge, he follows me at a distance to our suite.

"I'm going to take a nap," I inform him once he walks into the lounge.

He nods, walking over to the sofa to upload his pictures from the day.

I lock my door and slip over to the door to my balcony. Stepping out onto it, I see Conner already waiting for me by the pool. I hold my finger to my lips to keep him from saying anything.

After double-checking my bag to make sure I have my phone, wallet, and room key card, I carefully hug the pillar connecting my balcony to the first floor patio below it. Conner is there, his hands gripping my waist, as he eases me the rest of the way till my feet touch the ground.

"Are you sure about this?" he whispers, glancing up to my balcony.

"As I'll ever be." I grin, grabbing his hand and pulling him toward the main entrance.

A car is waiting for us to take us back to the falls and the Victoria Falls Border Bridge. We have day visas issued to make our way onto the bridge. We aren't going to Zimbabwe, but the bridge is considered a neutral zone between their borders.

"Do you want me to go with you?" Conner asks as we near the platform.

I shake my head. "I want to do this by myself."

He drapes his arm across my shoulders. "You'll be great. I'll take a bunch of pictures."

When we get to the platform, we get registered. The two young men working tell me to take off my jewelry, so I slip my earrings, giant watch, and charm bracelet into my bag. Conner holds it for me as I go first.

I have a momentary panic attack once I'm on the ledge. What if the cord breaks? What if I get hurt? I'm so scared that I can barely move. Arthur, our bungee jump assistant/psychiatrist, has clearly been in this situation before.

"You don't have to do this if you don't want to," Arthur calmly assures me, his hands covering the death grip I have on the railing.

I whimper. I want to do this. I just might cry while I do it.

From his experience, he must know my whimper means I still want to jump. He helps me to the edge of the platform and reminds me of what we covered during registration, or at least the highlights.

I glance back at Conner once I'm on the edge of the platform. He snaps a picture of what I'm certain will not show any type of game face. I have personally never considered bungee jumping in my bucket list of things I wanted to do. I'm here for

Ally. This is something she talked about wanting to try.

I think back to the bird crossing the falls this morning before I spread my own wings and leap. For a whole two seconds, my momentum takes me outward over the Zambezi River. I'm weightless. I'm free.

Then, I'm screaming my head off as I fall. Screaming is pointless as air rushes upward into my mouth before I clamp it shut. Having never fallen from such a height before, I am unprepared for how fast I fall. My eyes fail at absorbing the blur of the falls and foliage as I fall toward the rushing river. When I reach the full stretch of the bungee, I feel my body jerk upward, only for gravity to pull me down again.

The upward and downward jerk of the bungee is making me feel nauseous. As proud as I feel that I have done it and how close to Ally I feel in that moment, all I want to do is get back onto the bridge before I throw up into the river.

I try to push that feeling aside, to physically make myself be present in the beauty surrounding me. Taking as many mental pictures as I can, I feel the tug of being pulled back up to the platform.

"You did great." Conner congratulates me once I'm safely away from the edge.

He passes me my bag and asks if I can take some pictures of his jump. This is not his first time.

There's no whimpering and no hesitation when Arthur gives him the go-ahead to jump.

His initial leap is breathtaking. I snap picture after picture of his outstretched arms as his muscular legs propel him off the bridge. His face isn't always facing my direction as he falls, but I think I'm able to capture at least one shot of his expression. It's an expression of pure joy. I'm pretty sure he doesn't feel like throwing up.

Once he's back on the bridge, the first words out of his mouth are, "Want to go again?"

I can't help but grin. "Never again."

He holds my hand as we walk back to the Zambian border together. There's nothing romantic in the gesture. I just know, no matter where Conner and I end up in the world, I made a lifelong friend today.

Once we're on our way back to the lodge, Conner turns to me. "Think he knows you're gone yet?"

I cringe. "We'll find out soon enough."

His hand finds mine again as we make our way back into Royal Chundu.

Adam's back is to us as he is frantically speaking to someone at the front desk. The attendant, seeing us walking in, points in our direction.

Adam spins to face us, his eyes first finding mine before coming to rest on my hand in Conner's. "Where the fuck were you?"

Conner starts to say something, but Adam cuts him off. "I was asking Aubrey."

I straighten my shoulders and meet his gaze head-on. "I went bungee jumping."

Adam tilts his head to the side and blinks. The three of us stand there in an awkward standoff while Conner and I wait for Alex to respond. All he does is nod his head before turning on his heel and leaving Conner and me standing there.

I squeeze Conner's hand before dropping it to chase after Adam. I have to dig in my bag to find my key card.

"Aren't you going to say anything?" I glance around our lounge before marching into his room.

He's sitting on his bed with his back to me. His voice is low when he asks, "Do you have a death wish?"

I'm not sure if he means by bungee jumping or following him. "No."

He turns to look at me. "Why would you run off like that? In a foreign country? Do you even know if that place was safe?"

I sink into an armchair by his door. "Would you have let me go if I asked you?"

His shoulders sag. "I don't know. Maybe not."

When he drops his face into his hands, I jump up and rush over to him. I kneel in front of him and pull his hands down, so I can see his face. The look in his eyes haunts me.

"I didn't know where you were."

Whatever fun I originally convinced myself giving him the slip would be is gone now. I feel awful, knowing that I scared him. It was one thing in London. I was so annoyed at him, not that I haven't been annoyed at him since. It's just that I know he has my safety as his main concern.

"I won't do it again. I'm sorry. I just—"

He lifts me up into his lap and buries his face in my neck, effectively cutting me off. I have known him for only ten days. I don't know how to rest in his arms, his breath hot against my skin. The whiplash of emotions from him has rendered me incapable of understanding what I should do.

His breathing calms as he clings to me. When his breath becomes a soft tickle on my throat and not a hot gust, his arms loosen. I move to slip free from his grasp, resting my hand on his shoulder to steady myself. His hand reaches up to cover mine.

"Are you still upset with me?" I ask, standing between his legs.

He looks up at me, brown hair falling into his eyes, and he shakes his head. "Just promise me you'll talk to me before you go off on some dangerous date again."

"It wasn't a date," I argue.

He smirks at me, so I repeat myself.

"It wasn't a date."

He drops his hand from mine and puts his hands on my hips, gently pushing me a step backward, so he can stand. "I saw you two holding hands."

"He was just being supportive. It's not what you think."

He pushes his hair out of his eyes and looks at me, almost as though he's deciding whether to trust me or not. After today, I know I have given him no reason to trust me ever again.

He changes the subject, ushering me out of his room. "Did you like bungee jumping?"

"Not something I have any interest in ever doing again," I admit sheepishly. "Have you ever been?"

"Once, in Florida. I remember being exhausted after the adrenaline wore off."

His words are almost magical. As soon as he says them, I struggle to keep my eyes open. He almost smiles as he leads me across the lounge and into my room. I pause, seeing the door is open.

"The hotel manager has a key," Adam answers my unspoken question before sitting me on the edge of my bed.

I watch him, detached and half-asleep, as he sits me up, unzips my windbreaker and slips it off me. He then kneels at my feet and unties my sneakers before sliding them off my feet. I feel like a rag doll in his grasp as he lowers me until my head rests on my pillow. He eases the blanket from under me and gently tucks me in. The last thought that crosses my mind as he lowers the mosquito netting is how confusing this side of him is to the Adam I met in the lobby.

Too soon, the covers I'm hugging are being pulled from me as a bossy Adam attempts to wake me up.

"It can't be morning yet," I mumble, burying my face into my pillow.

"It's only been three hours."

I lift my head. "Why are you waking me up if it's only been three hours?" I can't be held responsible for the whine that accompanies my question.

He looks boyish and up to no good as he tugs on my arm. "Come on, you have to see this."

He helps me to a sitting position. I wipe sleep from my eyes as he tries to hurry me along.

"Do I need shoes?" I ask, each word punctuated by a yawn.

He starts to put my shoes on for me, but I push him away, already embarrassed because he tucked me in like a little girl earlier.

Once my shoes and windbreaker are back on, he leads me outside to the back of the lodge by the pool. I cringe, looking at the pillar I shimmied down during my escape, before he directs my attention skyward.

"It's called a moonbow." His breath tickles my ear. "The light from the moon is reflected off the mist of the waterfall."

The moon is full, the mist an arched halo over it.

"Beautiful," I breathe.

"I know," he agrees. Only, he's looking at me, not the moon.

I'm awake now.

We stand side by side for maybe fifteen minutes before I acknowledge the emptiness that is my stomach. "I'm going to head inside and grab a late dinner."

He turns to follow me. "I'll hang out with you."

I still feel guilty about earlier, so him being nice isn't helping. "You don't have to."

He almost smiles. "It's cool. I want to hear more about your adventure today."

The restaurant area is still open but not fully staffed. I order a simple chicken dish with the sauce on the side and some rice. I sip my water while we wait for it to come out.

After telling Adam about my jump, he asks, "The way you describe it, it doesn't seem like you wanted to do it. Why did you?"

I pause, not wanting to share the whole Ally thing with him. "Remember my tattoo?"

He nods. "How's it healing?"

I haven't needed to bandage it since the last time he did it. I've just rubbed cream on it a few times a day.

"It itches," I admit before continuing. "So, the tattoo was for my aunt. Bungee jumping was something she always wanted to do."

He drums his fingers on the tabletop before leaning toward me. "Both times you've run off, you were doing something for your aunt."

I dip my head in acknowledgment.

"Tattoos and bungee jumping…"

I nod.

"She must have been really cool."

I bite my lip as I try in vain to blink back the tears, but the floodgate opens, and they stream down my face.

"Shit," Adams says, pushing his chair closer to mine. He wraps his arm around my shoulder and tucks my face into his chest. "I didn't mean to make you cry."

"She was so cool." My words are muffled against his shirt.

As I cry, it hits me that he's stroking my hair, like he's petting me. I don't know why I find that so funny in that moment, him petting me, but I start to laugh. He must question my sanity as I laugh-cry on him. When I get the hiccups, it only makes me laugh harder.

His arms grip my shoulders as he pushes me backward to look at me. "Did you take anything with Conner?"

My mouth drops, and I promptly hiccup in his face.

"Are you on drugs?" he continues.

I drop my head to the table and cover it with my hands, mortified. "I haven't taken anything. I promise," I manage to get out between hiccups.

He rubs my back as I try to pull myself together. When I straighten, he offers me a napkin to dry my eyes.

"Were you laughing?" he asks cautiously.

I'm no longer laughing or crying, but the stray hiccup still plagues me. I look up at the ceiling, unable to look him in the eyes. "It felt like you were petting me, like a cat or dog, when you started to rub my hair. It caught me off guard."

I glance at him and he has the decency to look embarrassed. I mean, he was petting me.

"I was just trying to comfort you," he stammers.

I reach out to touch his arm. "You did. You made me laugh."

He sags back against his chair as my food comes out. I'm starving. I make no attempt to disguise my desire to shovel the entire plate into my mouth in one bite.

"You're hungry," he says dryly, watching me.

I nod, mouth too full to politely reply. I should be embarrassed. He is one of the most beautiful men I have ever seen close-up. I guess cry-laugh-hiccuping all over someone will remove fear of future embarrassment.

When I'm done eating, we walk back to our suite together. I email my parents while Adam uploads some pics from the trip to his Twitter page.

"Why don't you have a blog?" I ask, looking up from my phone.

"I like the one hundred forty character limit."

I don't tweet, so he turns his computer to me to show me what that means. Each tweet is kind of like a text message with a picture attached. Short and sweet.

He closes his laptop. "We have a long car ride ahead of us tomorrow. We should probably get some sleep."

Just thinking about where we're going tomorrow makes falling asleep seem impossible. It's a four hundred mile trip from Livingstone to the Kapani Lodge in the Luangwa National Park. We're going on safari.

FIFTEEN

Conner meets me in the morning, whispering in my ear that he's going to kiss my cheek to piss off Adam. We exchange email addresses, and I promise to keep him posted on our timeline on the off chance he can meet up with us when we reach Australia. In what seems to be great a personal strain, Adam manages to shake his hand and wish him well before we leave.

Crossing Zambia by car proves to be an adventure all on its own. The speed our driver goes varies from what feels like fifteen miles per hour to a time trial for NASCAR. At one point, we're stopped indefinitely as a herd of puku blocks our way. I look over at Adam, who's hanging out his window, camera in hand, taking pictures.

When we finally make it to the Kapani Lodge, all I want to do is get into our room and collapse into bed. That's until I see the room setup. The beds, while separate, are right next to each other with only an area wide enough to walk in between them. Maybe if they each had their own mosquito netting, it wouldn't look so intimate. Tonight and the two following it, Adam and I will be underneath the same net.

Suddenly feeling less tired, we make our way to the outdoor deck. I'm relieved when I see the menu with so many Western courses on it. Adam is adventurous and orders a local fare while I have a hamburger and french fries.

After dinner, we watch the sunset before going back to our room. I decide against telling my dad how this room is laid out. I know he assumes it's a suite with two separate rooms like the Royal Chundu. I get ready for bed first while Adam tries in vain to get a wireless signal.

He gives up, not wanting to keep me up, as he swears at his laptop under his breath. I'm pretending to read a book as I watch him walk from the bathroom over to our beds. He's shirtless, his basketball shorts hanging low on his hips. My mouth feels dry as I forgo my farce of reading, setting my book on the nightstand instead.

He starts untying the net around my bed first. He struggles with the first knot, his abs right at my eye level. He must notice I'm watching him.

"If you want to help, you can untie the netting around my bed."

I gulp, getting out of bed and making my way over to the far post of his bed. We work in parallel, moving from post to post, until we meet in the middle. He holds his netting up, so I can pass under it. He checks the edges, making sure there aren't any gaps, before getting into his bed. We lie there, each on our side, facing each other, neither moving to turn out the light.

I break the silence. "Kinda feels like we're camping, doesn't it?"

He looks up at the tent-like netting surrounding us. "It does. Do you like to camp?"

"I haven't been in forever. I remember liking it, but I think I was a girl scout the last time I did it."

He almost smiles. "You were a girl scout?"

I grin. "Don't sound so shocked. Were you a boy scout?"

He gets a faraway look in his eyes. "A long time ago." Then, he reaches over and turns out the light, promptly ending our conversation.

I lie there, my eyes adjusting to the now dark room. I consider saying something else, asking if he's still awake or something. Instead, I bite my tongue and let the sounds of the park around us lull me to sleep.

The bug-to-net ratio when I awake is significantly higher than my previous nights in Africa. There's a particularly large brown bug crawling upward right over my head.

"Adam," I breathe in a hushed whisper as though the sound of my voice might alert this giant bug that I am aware of its presence.

"Mmm," is all I get in reply as I hear the rustle of his sheets.

I keep my eyes on gigantor.

"Adam," I whisper again, just a fraction louder than the first time.

"Hmm?" The slight rise at the end of his mumble signifies a question.

"There's a really big bug on my net."

I hear more rustling and the sound of his feet touching the ground. My eyes are still locked on the slow upward trek of the bug. I squeak when Adam climbs on my bed, straddling me, to get a closer look at the bug. He moves the net around, so he can get a look at the backside of the bug. He looks down at me as I clutch my sheets to my chest.

"Harmless."

"Can you still get rid of it?" I plead.

His mouth twitches. He eases off my bed and puts on his sneakers before slipping under the net. He grabs a magazine from the top of the dresser and approaches the bug.

I sit up, eyes wide. "You aren't going to kill it, are you?"

He stops mid-stride and puts a hand on his hip. "No, I'm not going to kill it."

I feel too close to the bug and move over to Adam's bed. He shakes his head at me before sliding the magazine under the bug, between it and the net. Once it's all the way on the magazine, Adam calmly walks it over to the balcony and shakes it onto the railing.

He sets the magazine back where he found it before ducking back under the net. I'm still sitting on his bed. He looks at me and shrugs before stepping out of his shoes and into my bed. He flops onto his belly, burying his face into my pillow.

"That's my bed," I say, feeling silly for stating the obvious.

He turns his head, so he's facing me. "And you're on mine."

He's right. I am on his bed, the bed where he spent last night shirtless. I can't help myself. I lower myself until my head rests on his pillow. I face him.

He raises a brow. "Aren't you forgetting something?"

Does he want me to ask him for permission to be on his bed? "Can I lie on your bed?" I ask softly.

His eyes widen. "You never have to ask that."

My breath catches in my throat.

"I meant, are you going to thank me for getting rid of your bug?"

"Oh…" I half laugh, half stammer, feeling like an idiot. "Thank you, Adam."

I relax further onto his pillow, quietly inhaling his scent. What did he mean by I never have to ask? He wouldn't lie with me before.

After the bungee-jumping incident, I started feeling less annoyed by him. Since the first night I met him, I'd found him attractive, but his bossiness put me off. Am I starting to like him?

I peer over at him. His eyes are closed, and he looks like he's already fallen back asleep in my bed. I envy that—the ability to turn off your brain and just sleep.

Right now, looking at him, my mind races as I try to reconcile how I feel about him. My internal pro and con lists are interrupted by the sound of an alarm. I sit up and look on the bedside table as the noise gets louder.

Adam lifts his head from my pillow and squints at me. Recognizing the alarm, he moves from my bed to his, lying across my stomach. His head and arms reach to the other side of the bed.

I'm frozen. His weight is pinning me beneath him. Last night, he dropped his jacket and jeans on the floor next to the bed. He fishes his phone out of his pocket and turns off the alarm before inching off of me.

"Sorry about that," he manages, rubbing the back of his head.

I pull my knees to my chest, wrapping my arms around them. I look away when I say, "It's okay."

"Ready for a safari?" he asks, rubbing his hands together.

I nod. "Do you want the shower first?"

He leans back against my bed. "You can go first, so you can wake up," he teases.

I slide off his bed as he starts opening the net and using the ties around our bedposts to secure it.

I slip past him and grab my toiletry bag before heading to the bathroom.

I've just set everything out on the counter when I realize I forgot the shirt I'm going to wear today. I walk back out into our room and see him moving the pillow from my bed and switching it with the pillow from his.

He turns to see me watching him. His eyes are bold and unapologetic as he tells me, "I liked smelling you as I fell asleep."

I say nothing. I just walk over to my bag to fetch the shirt I forgot before speed walking back into the bathroom. To say I'm turned on is an understatement.

My solo shower might have been the most erotic of my life as I imagine his hands and his lips all over me. I touch myself, wishing he were in there with me. I bite my lip to keep from crying out as I shiver under the warm stream of water.

Knowing that he's waiting out there, I pull myself together and rush to get ready. I tug at my hair, willing it to grow long enough so that I can pull it back into a ponytail. Giving up, I tuck my hair behind my ears and walk back into our room.

Adam is standing over by his bed, taking clothes from his suitcase and putting them into a white garment bag. "Grabbed an extra one for you if you need any laundry done," he says, lifting another white bag.

"Thanks." I walk over to him and reach for the bag.

Getting laundry done for us is a giant perk of this lodge. He finishes loading up his bag before heading to the bathroom. I'm still in awe of how little time he needs to get ready.

We go have breakfast before meeting our tour guide. We ride in an open-top, almost military Jeep. Our guide carries a shotgun and rides in the front passenger seat. There's a couple on our tour sitting on the middle bench. Adam and I are behind them.

Chelle, the Mrs., turns around and asks us how long we've been together. Adam wraps his arm around me, pulling me closer to him, as he tells her we've been together for a year, and we're here to celebrate our first anniversary. I start to correct him, but he covers my mouth with his hand.

While the roads we travel aren't paved, they're smoothed by use. We head west toward a popular watering hole in search of zebra or elephants. Our only rule for the tour is to remain in the vehicle. They provide binoculars. I spend most of the tour looking through them, smacking Adam on the arm and pointing whenever I see something.

An hour into it, all we've seen are more puku, the same deer-looking animal we saw the day before on our way up to the lodge. Someone on a walkie-talkie directs the driver to head north.

My mouth drops as I see elephants through my binoculars. There are five of them—four large, one small. Our driver slowly brings us closer to them, keeping the front of the Jeep angled away from them. I assume it's in case they charge. We stay there for twenty minutes, watching them and taking pictures until the driver is notified that zebras are west of us. After the four hour tour we return to the lodge for a late lunch.

Adam is bummed because we didn't see any lions. I am more okay with not seeing any lions in the wild than I thought I would be. It's the elephants I really wanted to see. I can picture the image of them on Ally's Better board. Seeing them like how they were in her picture made me feel close to her.

I'm quieter than normal during lunch. Adam tries to get me to talk, but my thoughts are far away. I leave him to socialize with our guides as I go back to our room. I'm thrilled to see our laundry has already been returned. I start to unpack mine, but I end up lying down instead.

Our sheets were changed while we were on our safari. I don't know why this bugs me as much as it does. I expected to smell Adam on my pillow.

I'm reading my book when he comes in to check on me. I set it down and look up at him.

"Why did you tell that couple we were together?"

"It's just safer for you to have a boyfriend than to be single when traveling, so you can avoid unwanted attention."

"Unwanted attention?" I raise a brow.

He shrugs. "Trust me on it, okay?"

I nod. I'm not trying to argue. I'm just curious. He talks me into going back out with him. He says that there are a whole group of guests hanging out on the main deck.

As we leave the room, he grabs my hand. I give him a look, but he just squeezes my hand and doesn't say anything.

Chelle waves as we walk up. "What do you want to drink?" she asks as she signals an attendant.

I glance at Adam.

"Want a beer?" he asks, wrapping his arm around my waist and pulling me to his side.

"Sure. Whatever you're having, hon." I can play couple.

I watch as he orders us each a golden lager.

As the night goes on, we continue to be a charming couple. We share a table with Chelle and her husband, Matthew. After Adam playfully nips at my ear, my hand drifts down to rest on his thigh. His eyes widen, and I realize I'm not pretending. The thing is, I can't tell if he is or isn't. I lift my hand and put both of them on the table where I can see them before ordering water.

When we walk back to our room, he reaches for my hand again. Instead of just palming it, he laces his fingers through mine. I focus all of my mental power on not tripping and willing my hand not to sweat and/or feel clammy.

Chelle and her husband are a ways behind us. Their room is on the same floor. Instead of just opening our door, Adam turns me, so my back is to it as he presses up against me.

"What are you doing?" I gasp.

I shiver as he trails the tip of his nose from my earlobe down to my chin and then back again.

"Just making sure everyone sees you're taken."

I turn my head to see Chelle give us a thumbs-up before she and her husband slip into their room.

"No one is watching now."

His eyes bore into mine. "Do you want me to stop?"

I watch his tongue wet his lower lip as I lift mine to his in an answer to his question. His lips are soft, and his tongue instantly seeks entrance. I can taste him. I never want this kiss to end. My mind is screaming that this could end badly as my arms snake around his neck. With one hand pressed against our door, he coils the other around my waist, eliminating any negative space between us.

The hand attached to the arm wrapped around my waist tries in vain to open our door. A combination of his other hand pressing the door closed and the key card being backward are to blame. He breaks our kiss, and I whimper at the separation.

He opens the door and pulls me into it. His lips find mine again as the door swings shut behind us. He didn't shave this morning, so his scruff feels rough against my chin. I'm in sensory overload from him—his taste, the feel of his hands as they mold me to him, his scent that I mourned the loss of earlier that afternoon.

One of his hands slides up my back and into my hair. I laughed the last time he touched my hair. This time, I want to purr. He groans against my lips. I swallow the sound, taking it inside me.

We kiss our way across the room, and there's a moment's hesitation as he decides which bed we should fall into. He goes with his, pulling me down with him.

As my inner voice of reason rears its ugly head, I begin to wonder how many drinks Adam had as I doubt he could be into me in his own right mind. Do I just go with it? Not going with it doesn't seem physically possible. I want to climb him like a tree. God, and the way his hands feel on my body, there is nowhere else I want to be.

He pulls back, lifting himself off the bed. My mouth drops. Is he stopping? He catches my gaze, and his eyes scorch me. Our eye contact breaks as he pulls the hoodie he's wearing over his head, and he tosses it across the room. Underneath, he is wearing a faded T-shirt that fits snugly over his arms and chest. My fingers itch to pull it off of him,

216

but now, I feel the added heat my body doesn't need from my windbreaker. I reach for my zipper.

"Let me," he rasps, placing his hand over mine.

I surrender it to him, almost panting, as he lowers it in slow motion. I feel exposed despite my V-neck shirt as he parts my jacket and stares down at me hungrily. His hand slips under my neck, lifting me, as his other hand eases my jacket off one shoulder and then the other. As the material slides down my arms, I feel skinned, raw, a feast for him to consume.

He pounces, covering me again. Only this time, when I drag my fingertips across his back, I can feel the heat coming off of him through his shirt. My hips twitch, and his hand tightly grips my waist to stop me.

His hand moves up to brush my hair off my face. His eyes are tender as he lowers his lips to mine. His hand moves from my hair to cup my face. He's slowing us down. I feel relieved and disappointed at the same time. I'm not naive, but it's been a while, and I just assume it hasn't been for Adam.

"This is wrong," he breathes against my lips before his tongue caresses mine. "I'm supposed to be looking out for you," he continues, his lips moving to taste my neck.

"You are looking out for me," I argue, arching my back and pushing against his hand as it moves from my waist to mold my breast.

I push my chest further into his hand. I want him with every fiber of my being, and I panic as his movements continue to slow.

He rests his forehead against mine. His gray eyes slay me. "Aubrey, what are we doing?" His words drip with remorse, quelling the passion that pooled within me.

But it doesn't stop me from blurting out, "I want you."

His eyes close as he inhales, stealing all the air around us. He rolls to the side, falling off of me, to lie next to me. "I want you too."

I don't understand the frustration in his tone. We both want each other.

"Why did you stop?" I roll toward him, reaching out to turn his face to look at me.

When he flinches from my touch, I slowly pull my hand back and sit up, my back to him.

"I'm trying to do the right thing."

My shoulders sag as I glance back at him. "What about being with me is so wrong?"

"I feel like I'm taking advantage of you," he says.

I stand and turn on him. "I am not a child."

He reaches his hand out to me. "That's not what I said."

I push his hand away and glare at him. "Don't."

"Aubrey, come on," he pleads.

"No. All you did tonight was mess with my head. You clearly need to figure some stuff out."

I turn and walk to the bathroom, needing to be away from him to pull myself back together. I just cannot understand why he even kissed me in the first place if he thought it was wrong. He's here with me to help me make sure I don't get lost while moving between countries. He's not my babysitter. I close the door behind me and lean against the sink counter. I gaze up at my reflection to see my swollen lips and my chin reddened from his stubble.

Turning the cold tap, I splash water on my face. I'm surprised I'm not crying. I should be feeling rejected right now. Instead, I'm pissed. Whatever happened tonight, he started.

Now, I have to exist knowing what his lips feel like on mine and that he thinks it's wrong somehow. I despise our shared quarters more than ever now. I do not want to sleep under our tent-like netting with him. I don't want to watch his chest rise and fall as he sleeps. I also would rather walk across hot coals than seek his aid in large bug removal. What I need is my own room, the privacy to nurse my wounds alone and not under his watchful eye.

Knowing I can't avoid him forever, I walk back into our room. I need to change for bed. I should have grabbed my things on the way to the bathroom. I don't want to go in there again. I don't want him to think I was hiding.

Anger fuels me on as I change in front of him, my back turned. Maybe I think I can show him what he's missing out on, what he decided is wrong. I slip off my jeans, knowing my shirt almost covers me. Almost. If I were truly brave, I would have taken my shirt and bra off before putting on the yoga pants I sleep in. I still feel a thrill, taking my shirt and bra off, my bare back to him.

"Aubrey, are you going to talk to me?"

I glance at him, over my naked shoulder. I try to look disinterested. "What do you want me to say?"

He licks his lips, looking up at the ceiling, before looking back at me. "Are you angry at me?"

My head dips back as I scoff. "I'm not happy with you."

I bend down to grab my T-shirt and drag it over my head, feeling somehow powerful in being unafraid of changing in front of him.

"I feel really bad—"

I turn on him fully, cutting him off, "You feel bad for kissing me? Shit, Adam. You can be a real asshole."

His mouth drops.

I continue, "You made it crystal clear that you think kissing me is wrong. That's awesome, really great, because I didn't. So, now knowing how much of a mistake you thought it was sucks. Should be fun playing the happy couple tomorrow, seeing as how I don't even want to look at you right now.

If it's cool with you, instead of me having to listen to you say again how kissing me was a mistake, I'd like to go to bed. Do you have any issues with that?"

I take a step back when he charges me, pulling me hard against him and putting his lips on mine.

I push him away, gasping. "What the hell are you doing?"

He traps me, the post of my bed at my back. "Maybe I don't care anymore if this is wrong."

He dips his face toward mine, but I turn my head.

"Maybe I care that you thought it was." He takes a step back, raking his fingers through his hair. "I feel responsible for you. There—I said it. But trust me, I do not think you are a child. I'm shit at this, and I am only trying to save you from me."

I push off the post and walk over to sit down on my bed, putting my elbows on my knees and rubbing my temples. He follows me but sits on his bed, right across from me, our legs almost touching.

I'm trying to process what he said. I can't be too offended that he feels responsible for me. It's annoying, yes, but I respect that he's honest about it.

He wants to save me from himself? I just don't understand what he means by that.

So, I ask, "Why do you think you need to save me..." I pause, looking up at him. "From yourself?"

He rolls his shoulders. "I'm not looking for a relationship, Aubrey."

I fold my arms across my chest. "Who says I am?"

He rubs the pad of his index finger back and forth across his lips. I wonder if he can still taste me. We seem locked in some strange staring contest. I'm waiting for him to make a move even though I'm not sure how I'll react. Part of me feels as though whatever moment we had is lost. To begin again, at this moment, would feel forced. The way he stopped us before bruised my ego and broke whatever spell we were under.

It feels like forever before he speaks. "Well, I sure fucked this up."

I cover my mouth, trying in vain to hold in my laughter. His words break whatever tension lingered. He looks a bit wounded that I'm laughing.

"I'm sorry. I wasn't expecting you to say that. Look, it's been an interesting night. Let's just try to get some sleep."

He nods his head and slowly makes his way to the bathroom. I try in vain to fall asleep before he comes back. I stay in my bed as he loosens our netting from the posts and carefully drapes them around our beds. I'm startled when he comes to my bed and not his.

I start to say something, but he beats me to it. "Can I just lie with you? We don't have to do anything. I just…I just want to lie with you."

I'm about to say that I don't think it would be a good idea, but his rasped, "Please," kills my opposition.

I move to the side, making room for him, only to be pulled back until I'm flush against him, my back to his bare chest. His arms surround me. I'm disappointed in myself at how quickly I surrender.

I lie stiffly in his arms at first. I'm overanalyzing what this means and how my acceptance of him being in my bed makes me look. I wonder if he's going through the same thing I am until I hear the gentle change of breathing that signals he's asleep.

Even though sleep evaded me prior to him joining me, the rhythmic cadence of his breathing lulls me to sleep. My last coherent thought is acknowledging the feel of his arms tightening around me.

SIXTEEN

At some point overnight, we shift.

When I awake, my cheek is resting on his shoulder with my nose at his neck, our limbs tangled. I know I should slip away. It would be the easiest way to avoid any awkwardness over last night. It hurt when he pulled away.

I've just made up my mind to ease myself from his grasp when I feel his body shift. He lifts the arm I'm not lying on above his head and groans as he stretches, his chest pushing out toward me. My hands almost reflexively reach up to brace myself. He pauses mid-stretch to look down at me before pouncing. I'm on my back, my hands pinned above my head.

Adam's face hovers over mine. "What do we have here?"

"Adam!" I exclaim, startled.

He tilts his head to the side, almost smiling. "No, I'm Adam. You're Aubrey."

I flex my fingers and glare at him when he doesn't release me. "I'm thrilled you're in such a good mood this morning. Wanna let me go now?"

He sighs, letting go of my wrists and sitting up on his heels, straddling me.

I push up on my elbows. "Are you going to move?"

His hand moves to the hem of my shirt, pushing it up a couple of inches to expose my stomach, before I swat at it.

He rubs the hand I hit. "Thought we should do some exploring today."

I tug my shirt back down. "Fun as that sounds, it would probably be smarter if we didn't."

He shifts his weight off of me and lies back down next to me. "But I thought..." He trails off.

I turn onto my side, facing him. "You were right to stop last night. It wouldn't be a good idea for us to get involved. Things could get awkward. Feelings, probably mine, could get hurt. I think we should just stay friends."

He gives me a look.

"Or become friends. Whatever," I amend.

He gets up, pushing the netting back and tying one side up to the post of his bed, before walking over to his bag. He walks back and drops a small bag onto my stomach. "All right, friend, I meant to give you this earlier. It's no big deal. I'm going to go shower."

I sit up all the way. "What is it? Don't you want to watch me open it?"

He shrugs and leans against the post of my bed. I smooth the comforter out in front of me and shake the contents of the bag out onto it. Out tumble two charms—a small bottle of wine or maybe beer and a waterfall. In all of the excitement, I forgot to get charms for my bracelet.

I'm blinking away tears when I look up to thank him.

He avoids my eyes, "It's nothing."

But I know better. I set the charms on the table between our beds before getting up and going to him.

I answer the question on his lips with my kiss. I know he can hurt me, but now, I know I can hurt him too, and somehow, that comforts me. He doesn't argue. He just accepts my surrender, lifting me and carrying me back to my bed. His lips leave mine briefly as he walks to, and then digs through his bag for something.

I need his touch before I lose my mind. "What are you looking for?"

His head stays down as he continues to search for something. "I know I have a condom."

Oh. "Adam…"

Something in my tone compels him to look up at me.

"I'm on the pill. I'm clean. If you are too, we don't have to use one. I trust you."

He closes his eyes and takes a deep breath before he comes to me, pausing only to free the netting until it surrounds us once more.

Adam makes good on his earlier teasing. He explores me. His deft hands make short work of my clothes. With his mouth and his hands, he erases the memory of every other touch I knew. Some people believe the Garden of Eden was in Africa. I'm his garden, and he's my Adam, the first.

I pull at his shorts, and he pulls back to remove them. My gaze is bold as I watch him bare himself to me. My touch seems to hold a power over him as well. Even as sweat glistens on his brow, a gentle sweep of my fingertips makes him shiver.

When I push aside the hair falling forward onto his face, I see my reflection in his eyes, and I feel beautiful. My desire makes me desperate as I pull him toward me, lifting my hips to meet him. Any control he had before that is gone. He marks me, deep inside, over and over again.

Haphazardly throwing on his clothes from the day before, Adam leaves just once to get us food and chilled drinks. Shedding his clothes once he's back in our room, he proudly presents what he's gathered.

We make a picnic over on his bed, using our hands to feed each other, our hunger for each other only increasing as we eat. He trails pieces of mango across the tops of my shoulders, nibbling and licking its wake. Where he seems obsessed with my skin, I can't seem to get enough of the taste of his lips, his tongue.

He accepts my kisses greedily, pushing our picnic aside and tugging me into his lap. Our bodies were made to be joined, and we relax into each other. I slowly rock my hips, and his hands lift and lower me. We connect again. Our kiss only breaks as we cry out together.

My forehead falls to his shoulder, exhaustion taking over. I mumble complaints as he lifts me, ducking us both under the netting.

Adam carries me to our bathroom. He sets me on a small wooden stool by the vanity, and I droop as I watch him fill the large garden tub. As the water runs, he comes to crouch in front of me, lifting his hand to cup my cheek. Instinctively, I lean into his touch. Tub half-full, he reaches for my hand, and together, we settle into it. I'm nestled between his legs, my back to his chest.

Using a small dish meant to hold decorative soap, he wets my hair. My shampoo sits within arm's reach, and I drift off to sleep as he massages some into my scalp.

When I awake in bed for the second time that day, I'm once again tangled up in Adam. Only, it isn't the same. I'm naked in his arms, his bare body surrounding me. I feel changed. The clumsy lovemaking of my high school boyfriend did not prepare me mentally and physically to comprehend what it is to be worshiped intimately by a man.

I can lightly smell the scent of my body lotion on my skin. Somewhere between the bath and bed, he rubbed me down. I pout, sad I wasn't awake to enjoy it.

I watch Adam as he sleeps, and I wonder what this will mean for the remainder of our trip. He was upfront last night. He doesn't want a relationship. Is this a onetime event? Or will we continue as lovers? I'm now craving his body more than ever before, I fear there's a chance I don't have the same effect on him.

When I can no longer ignore my bladder, I all too easily slip free of his hold. I duck under the netting, and then I walk naked and unashamed to the bathroom.

I'm finger combing my now dampened hair when I hear him frantically call out my name.

I peek my head out the door, now suddenly shy. "Yes?"

Even through the netting, I can see how wild his eyes are until they settle on me. He drops his head into his hands, his shoulders shaking. I hurry over to him, pulling the netting to the side to get to him. He straightens only long enough to fold me into his arms. He buries his face into my neck, and my arms are around his shoulders.

"Shh," I soothe. "I'm right here."

His voice breaks as he says, "I dreamed you were hurt, and I couldn't..." He shudders. "And then, I woke up, and you were gone. I have to take care of you."

"Adam, look at me."

Stormy gray eyes reluctantly meet mine. I hold his gaze, my fingertips tracing his jawline on both sides, until his breathing calms. His grip around me tightens as he drops his lips to my neck.

"Wait," I plead, stopping him. "What happened?"

He shakes his head against my neck, his stubble lightly scratching my skin.

With the palms of my hands, I push against his shoulders. "Please tell me."

He lifts my hands before tugging me back closer to him. "I lost someone once, someone I was supposed to be watching out for."

I don't know what to say. I do the only thing I can think of to take his mind off whatever happened. I pull his lips to mine. He hesitates briefly before surrendering to me.

This time, I'm the one with complete control. I push his shoulders back until he rests against the pillows before I sink down onto him. Our hands clasp, our eyes lock, until the storm in his subside. With that, a familiar glint appears, my melancholy Adam gone. I'm flipped onto my back as Adam, the first man, begins his worship.

"Do you still want to go?"

I've grown too used to the feel of his arms around me. I absentmindedly trace the nail beds of his fingers, trying to make up my mind.

Finally, I glance back at him. "I'm a little scared."

He pushes my hair aside to look into my eyes. "The guides will have guns, and it's almost the same route we took yesterday."

I gulp. "But it's dark outside."

He folds my hands into his and kisses my cheek. "I'll protect you."

"Okay," I whisper.

We shower together, perhaps nervous about leaving the Eden we created today. Once dressed and ready, fingers interlaced, we walk to the patio to join the other guests for dinner. Chelle raises her glass and winks as we walk in. I laugh, not really caring. They all assume we're a couple anyway.

Over dinner, Adam sets up our night ride. We'll leave shortly after dinner and be back at the lodge three hours later. Our goal is to see the lions hunt. I'm going for Adam more than myself.

I feel like he needs me near him right now. I also guiltily think of Ally for the first time today, thinking she would have been disappointed in me if I'd let my fear hold me back.

I'm shaking in the seat next to Adam, so he tucks me in closer to his side. Our Jeep creeps at a slower pace than it moved the day before. I don't know if it's because of the visibility or to avoid scaring off the lions.

I think the moon and stars were bright the night Adam pulled me out to look at the moonbow. Away from the lodge, they seem even brighter even though the night is slightly overcast.

We have binocular-type, night-vision viewers. I don't like them. It takes a few moments for my eyes to focus when I stop looking out of mine. It scares me, making me feel like a lion or something else can sneak up on me in those moments, and I wouldn't know.

Our Jeep stops, slightly elevated, looking out over a wide grassy expanse. In hushed tones, the driver and the other man point toward something I can't see.

Adam hurriedly sets up his tripod on the seat on the other side of him, mumbling something about aperture and the light being good this close to sunset. He asks that we all sit still, so the camera won't shake. The guides seem used to this kind of request.

I feel vulnerable, scared something will come up from behind us. I cave and resort to using the night-vision viewers again. My heart thumps so wildly that I'm certain it's going to shake the Jeep and ruin Adam's pictures.

There, in the grass below us, the cats feed. We missed the hunt but observe the feast. I want to look away, the gore is too much for me, but I know his lens are trained on the carnage.

What seems like forever later, Adam exhales, and his shoot is over. Our guides offer to take us by a watering hole that's had a lot of crocodile activity. Adam takes one look at my face and declines. On our slow trek back to the lodge, he reminds me with a whispered kiss beneath my ear that there are still crocodiles in Australia.

Back at the lodge, we retreat into our room and our netted garden. We ready our bags for our morning departure before undressing each other for bed. We don't make love that night. Instead, we drift off to sleep, chest-to-chest, with my head tucked under his chin.

The next morning, I'm sad to leave our little Eden. I wonder if the magic we created will be lost as we move on to India. I briefly consider if I should leave some of Ally's ashes at the Kapani Lodge, but then I decide instead to keep that stop in my heart for just Adam.

I sleep on the long journey to the airport. Our flight takes us to a larger regional airport that then takes us to New Delhi. From there, a hired car takes us to our hotel in Agra, from the lodge it was a nineteen-hour journey.

Thankfully, our suite-style hotel room is air-conditioned. It's similar to the Royal Chundu by the falls. Adam ignores his room altogether, putting his things next to mine.

There's a rooftop restaurant where he goes to grab us food from while I shower and change. I tried to sleep on the plane but just couldn't get comfortable.

Showered, changed, and sprawled out across a queen-sized bed feels life-changing. I'm dozing when Adam walks in a while later.

"You'll be starving later if you don't eat something," he whispers, nibbling at my ear to wake me.

I groan, wishing he would just snuggle up to me and go to sleep instead. He takes a quick shower while I convince myself to get up. I make it as far as the lounge when he walks out, still damp, basketball shorts riding low on his hips.

"Did you ever play?" I ask, gesturing toward his shorts.

He shakes his head, unpacking the boxes and making each of us a plate. "I was overweight through most of school."

My jaw drops as he passes me my plate. I try to play off my reaction, but he sees it.

"When I lost my mom, I started using food as a way to make myself feel better. I was young, and my dad seemed on board. We gained weight together."

I smile down at my plate when I see he's gotten me simple brown rice and sweet bread, but

I pause when I think about the hard time he gave me about food in London. "Why would you tease me about being a picky eater?"

"You were fun to tease. Plus, I still think it's good to try different things, just in moderation."

He holds out his plate, showing me the different things he's trying. I do my best not to laugh at his pained expression when he tries the spiciest portion of his plate.

"How did you lose the weight?"

I'm surprised at the thunderclouds that shadow his gray eyes briefly as he's pulled somewhere in his mind.

After a moment, he simply replies, "It was time to change."

I'm either too tired or cautious to push it.

After we eat, we crawl into bed. Our hunger now for each other. This place is so different from our luxuriously rustic Eden, surrounded by almost untouched nature. Now, we're in one of the most populated countries in the world. Instead of birdsong, we hear the faint sounds of a Bollywood film coming from a TV in the room next to ours. Gone is the romantic tent-like netting that made our last room feel so isolated.

Even though everything else has changed, we're still the same. I'm relieved, and I give myself to him fully. Part of me stops feeling truly alive unless he's within me.

This night, my back is to his chest, and his body covers mine. I lose myself when I feel his lips dust my tattoo. The power he wields over my body leaves me breathless. His obsession with my skin hasn't dulled. His hands and lips never rest in their exploration of me. I take my time exploring him as well.

Before sleep can take us, I reward his gallant act of fetching us dinner with a neck and shoulder rub. He sits quietly, head drooped, as my fingertips search to bring relief to whatever tension I can find living there. With my bare legs bent on either side of him, he can't resist pulling my feet into his lap. As I massage him, he rubs them, both of us helping the other to rid any lingering soreness from our travels.

My time reveling in touching him is cut short after I lightly trace his tattoo and kiss it. He turns, pinning me beneath him, and takes my mouth in his. There's an urgency there that I don't understand, but I rise to meet it.

"God, Aubrey, what are you doing to me?" he groans against my lips as he plunges into me.

His lips steal any opportunity that I have to respond. I can barely breathe, but if I pass out, I'll be tasting his lips. A release I don't feel coming shudders through me, pulling him over as well. We lie there, panting and staring at each other, wide-eyed.

He tucks a strand of hair behind my ear. "I didn't see you coming."

I start to ask him what that means, but he shakes his head, dipping his lips to mine and sweetly kissing me.

SEVENTEEN

It might seem silly, but with my mom's help before the trip, I bought a ring especially for my visit to the Taj Mahal. Security is tight, and I don't want to have to explain Ally's ashes to them. So, instead of my little plastic container, I have an old pillbox ring. I won't be able to bring as much of Ally as I want, but I know this place is special to her. I leave the rest of Ally's ashes in our room.

I also don't want to get so lost in Adam that I forget the real reason I'm on this trip in the first place. I need to find myself and take time to say good-bye.

Out of all the places in the world, Ally always wanted to visit India in particular. There's something so exotic and romantic about it, especially the Taj Mahal. She wanted to see its reflection across the pools for herself.

The idea always seemed so romantic to me—a memorial built to the love of your life. It also makes me wonder how the Emperor Shah Jahan's other wives felt about it.

The area around the Taj Mahal is considered pollution-free, so no cars are allowed near it.

August in India is still oppressively hot. Our plan for our days in the country is to visit the places we want to see early in the day and be back in our room before the sun makes it uncomfortably hot.

We hire a rickshaw to take us there. Only, the driver keeps trying to take us shopping instead, pissing off Adam. We were warned prior to coming to India that anyone who tries to lead you to a certain shop is probably getting some sort of commission.

I know Adam is just excited to start taking pictures. Architectural elements seem to be his favorite things to take pictures of. He still enjoys the shots he took in Africa. It's just that he's more inspired by human creation than natural scenes.

I think it has to do with feeling in control. He can examine and capture the pieces of a building and understand how they came together. Nature, while beautiful, is unpredictable. Adam likes control.

When he reaches for my hand, I pause, looking around. Aren't there rules against public displays of affection? "Are we allowed?"

He actually smiles. "Yes, Aubrey. We're allowed to hold hands, anything more probably not."

Despite the heat, in case we have time to see the mosques, I'm wearing a long maxi skirt and a long-sleeved lightweight cotton shirt. Once we're through security and have our water and shoe covers, we pull out our phones. We both have walking tours of the Taj Mahal uploaded to them.

We hold hands, pausing whenever Adam wants to take some pictures, and we make our way around the grounds. At one point, as I watch him taking some pictures, it hits me that no one perfect shot or angle can truly capture its beauty. I wonder if this wasn't a tomb, if it would still feel sad. A famous poet called the Taj Mahal "a teardrop on the cheek of time."

We're not allowed to take pictures inside the mausoleum, but Adam takes many up-close pictures of the inlay stonework outside. The white marble is so bright against the blue sky.

Depending on the angle, it almost hurts to look directly at it. As numbers of workers and years of construction fill my thoughts, I try to imagine the Taj Mahal as it was being built. The emperor had planned a mirror-image black tomb to sit across the river, but his son stopped him. I'm almost happy that happened because the emperor is now buried with his wife here.

Adam has me sit on a bench, so he can take my picture with the tomb behind me. I rest my ring hand on top of my other on my lap. Then, he sits next to me, holding his camera out to get both of our faces in the shot. A person walks by and offers to take a picture for us, but he declines, leery of handing his pretty expensive camera to a stranger. I stay on the bench, turning to look back at the iconic view. Adam gets up to go look at something near us.

Throughout the day, I struggle with where to release Ally's ashes. There are beautiful, elaborate gardens all around the grounds, but none of them feel right. I decide there, on that bench, in that unwatched moment, that Ally should have that view of the Taj. I bend down and pretend to adjust the strap of my sandal, but I slowly spill her ashes instead. The small gray hill they form is so different from the previous ones. I lay my hand on top of them, pressing them into the ground beneath me, and I make her one with this place.

We walk to the small gift shop and find another charm for my bracelet. Just outside the shop, Adam hooks it on for me. I now have five charms on my bracelet, and I feel comfort in its weight on my wrist. The heat begins to bother both of us, so we bid farewell to the Taj not long after.

We head back to our hotel, and we are happy to eat the food from the night before. I change into shorts and an old T-shirt and nap while Adam uploads and edits pictures on his computer.

I'm just starting to wake up when he crawls into bed with me.

"Stay with me," he pleads, pulling me closer.

I turn, wrapping my arms around his neck. "You should have taken a nap first."

He buries his face in my neck. "I know."

I laugh, pulling back to look at his sleepy face. "Did you get all your pictures uploaded and edited?"

His eyes close as he nods. "Most of them."

I figure a longer nap isn't such a bad idea, and I settle down into his arms.

When we awake, he shows me pictures from the trip so far. I've seen the ones from London already, but it's fun to think back to the other places we've visited, the things we've seen. Since the hotel has Wi-Fi, I have him email some of my favorite ones to me, so I can send them in an email to my parents. Guilt is the main reason I email. I don't want them to worry, and I haven't sent them anything in a while.

I look at my watch, trying to figure out the time difference, when I realize I never changed the time zone to Agra. "Have you seen my manual?" I ask, digging through my bag.

He walks over to me and unhooks my watch from my wrist. "I think you should lose the watch."

I watch as he drops it into my suitcase. "But how will I know what time it is?"

He clears his throat and pulls his phone out of his pocket.

I duck my head, resting my forehead against his chest. "Oh my God, I'm a dumbass."

He slips his phone back into his pocket and rubs my back with both hands. "Happens to all of us."

I rest my cheek flat against his chest. "We're halfway done, you know."

His hands pause for a moment before they begin again. "I know."

I peer up at him. "So, what should we do now?"

He tilts his head to the side. "We could walk around and find a place to have dinner."

Though slightly wrinkled, my clothes from earlier are still clean. I change into them, and we hold hands as we walk around Agra. We stay near our hotel, not wanting to have a long walk back. I check out a few shops, finding a pretty purple sari to bring home for my mom and a green one for myself.

We have dinner. I don't eat much. The least spicy dish is still too much for me. When we get back to our hotel, Adam runs up to get me sweet bread from the rooftop restaurant. I surprise him by changing into my sari while he's gone. My food is forgotten once he's back, his full attention on unwrapping me.

I wake up the next morning to him playing with my hair. I squint up at him. "Having fun?"

He nods, pushing some into my eyes. I smooth it back before reaching to tousle his hair.

"A few years ago, my hair was closer to your length," I admit.

He reaches out to run his fingers through my hair again, not messing it up this time. "Why so short?"

I close my eyes, partly because what he's doing feels good and also because I'm not sure if I can talk about Ally and not get upset. "My aunt had chemo and started losing her hair, so my parents and I shaved our heads."

His fingers move down to trace the wings on my back. "This aunt?"

I nod. "Ally."

"Do you want to talk about her?"

I turn onto my back and look up at the ceiling. "I just miss her." I glance over at him. "This trip was supposed to be for her."

He looks at me confused, so I go on. "While she was sick, we planned this amazing trip she would take when she got better. She left the trip for me to take instead after she died."

"I had no idea," he says, shaking his head.

"I know." I laugh dryly. "I heard you that first night in the hallway, telling someone about the spoiled girl you were stuck with."

He drops his forehead to the pillow. "Wow. I was a total asshole, wasn't I?"

I hold my index finger and thumb up to show how much of an asshole I thought he was, giggling when he acts like he's going to bite my hand.

Not long after, he goes off in search of breakfast while I get ready. After breakfast, we hire

245

a car to take us to see the Chausath Khamba. It has all of these domes, but they're reversed, and the monument has a flat roof.

Adam is in heaven. He takes a ton of pictures, sometimes focusing on the minutest details.

From there, we have a car take us to John William Hessing's tomb, also known as the Red Taj Mahal. It's within a Roman Catholic cemetery. I have some of Ally's ashes with me, not that she ever spoke of this place. She didn't. I only discovered it while planning the trip with my mom.

It's nowhere near as big or grand as the real Taj Mahal, but something about it intrigues me. It was commissioned by a wife of a Dutch soldier after his death. It was built with red sandstone and mimics the original Taj Mahal.

It's missing the four towers though. The wife ran out of money before it was finished. I hope it's someplace Ally will enjoy being. I think she would have loved the romance of the story and the idea that it's not as well known.

It's surrounded by other graves, some larger than others. Some markers aren't unlike the gravestones of a modern day U.S. cemetery. There's also a grouping of domed structures to the one side of Hessing's tomb. It's here where I sit, legs crossed, and I spread Ally's ashes.

Adam is off somewhere, taking pictures. I think this spot is pretty, and I like that there's some shade, probably more for me than for Ally. I'm not sure what to do or what to say. I finally decide to tell her about Adam. I speak quietly since there are other people around, not many, but I don't want to look crazy. I set a sheet of paper on the ground in front of me that I can plausibly say I'm reading if anyone hears me.

It just feels right to talk to her about the boy in my life. I tell her what he looks like and what a pain in my ass he was in the beginning. I admit to her that I did some things I'm not proud of, particularly sneaking off the two times. I tell her what his kisses feel like and how sometimes I feel breathless in his arms. I look around to make sure I'm still alone when I tell her I'm scared that I'm falling for him. My hand still rests on her earthly remains. It's then when I feel the power of how gone she is.

If she were here, it would be now that I would ask for her advice. A cooling breeze kicks up, ruffling my hair and pushing the oppressive heat that led me to sit in the first place away from me. I'm not sure why, but I feel her presence so strongly in this moment. She's the breeze all around me. She's so close, but I still can't hug her. It's not enough, but since it's all I have, I close my eyes and try to feel her with all I have.

When the moment passes and I no longer feel her, I open my eyes to see Adam standing off a ways, watching me. I flex my hand, mentally giving Ally all my love, before standing up to go meet him. He sees me coming and moves toward me as well.

"Get some good pictures?" I ask.

He reaches for my hand, his thumb brushing over the top of it. He ignores my question. "You okay? You looked so sad a minute ago."

I turn my head, tucking a strand of hair behind my ear. "Being in a cemetery just made me think about Ally."

He squeezes my hand. "That makes sense. Will some sweets cheer you up?"

I look back at him. "What?"

"Some guy back that way told me we're crazy if we haven't tried any of the famous Agra sweets."

"Well, what are we waiting for?"

Our car picks us up from the hotel to take us back to the airport in New Delhi. From there, we're headed to China.

We have a layover in Shanghai, but it's the kind where we just wait on the plane. I use this time to try to get Adam to open up more about his past.

I lay my head on his shoulder, placing my hand atop his as it rests on my leg. "What made you decide to lose the weight?"

I can hear his slight intake of air as he processes my question. After a long pause, he says, "It just got in the way."

"Are you ever going to tell me?"

He rests his cheek on top of my head. "It's just not something I talk about."

I let it go, relaxing against him for the remainder of our journey. When we land in Beijing and after going through health, quarantine, and immigration, we find out my luggage is missing.

"But we never even changed planes," I try in vain to stress to the agent at the customer service desk for our airline.

My tears confuse Adam. He tries to tell me everything will be all right and anything I had can be replaced. I can't tell him right there about Ally's ashes. I'm beside myself as I watch Adam give the airline clerk our hotel information in case my luggage turns up. He doesn't understand why I don't want to leave, why I want to stay, and why I want them to let me search the plane myself. He even gets annoyed at me when I start crying in the baggage claim area.

It's not until we're in the taxi on the way to the hotel when I tell him that Ally's ashes are in there. He slides across the backseat and pulls me into his arms.

"I am so sorry. I didn't know." He squeezes me. "If you want, we can go back and make sure they're searching for your luggage."

He's only half-serious. We both know the airline wouldn't do anything differently if we were there. It just makes me feel a little better that he offers.

The taxi ride to the hotel is a blur. It's late, I'm upset, and I'm not that interested in Beijing at the moment. I stand off to the side while Adam checks us in at the hotel.

Not caring about the time difference, I call my parents when we get up to our room. I know they won't be able to do anything. I just need to hear their voices. Adam goes down to the gift shop to get us food to snack on. We completely skipped dinner, except for the fruit the room came stocked with.

"I don't think I can eat anything," I admit, feeling sick from not knowing where my bag is.

"Maybe a drink?" he asks cautiously.

It only reminds me of conversations I had with Ally, trying to get her to eat before she died. He watches me with an expression of confusion as I dissolve into fresh tears. How can he know that trying to get me to eat will only remind me of her? I know I'm poor company. It doesn't stop me from being upset. Adam still tries to distract me.

He eventually gives up, and we fall asleep apart for the first time in days.

When I awake the next morning, Adam is not asleep next to me. But somehow my luggage is in front of me. I tear into it, looking for the wooden box that holds Ally's ashes. Adam watches quietly from across the room as tears of relief stream down my face. After wiping my tears away, I motion for him to come and sit by me.

"How?" I look at him.

"I went down to the front desk. The airline had found your luggage and sent it right over."

I hug Ally's ashes to my chest and close my eyes. Silly as it seems, I introduce him to Ally. He doesn't seem uncomfortable or weirded out by it. Now that I no longer need to hide her box, I rest her by the window.

I can finally relax and appreciate the coolness of our room. The Emperor, our hotel, overlooks the pagodas of the Forbidden City. Even though it's surrounded by all of this history, it has a decidedly modern Ikea-ish feel. Our room has white and sage green as the accent color scheme. There's a line mimicking the skyline of the Forbidden City painted onto the green strip of paint that breaks up one wall.

On the way to breakfast, I notice the buttons in the elevator are in English too. We have breakfast on the rooftop deck before walking over to the Forbidden City. It was once a palace but is now an incredible museum. We spend most of the day looking at paintings, jade pieces, and Ming Dynasty vases.

Adam can't stop taking pictures of the buildings and the pagoda-topped towers. We spend part of the afternoon in the gardens until we have to stop for a late lunch. My feet are sore even though I'm wearing comfortable sandals.

We stumble across an unexpected gem of a restaurant near Jingshan Park. There's a beautiful courtyard lined with small red statues on the sides and black ones haphazardly across the middle. They come just below my knee and are all slightly different.

We feel slightly underdressed once we enter the main building, but the staff is so accommodating that we feel instantly at ease. They speak English, which relaxes me because I know I can trust what I'm ordering. The food is expensive, but the experience is worth it. There are multiple courses and unexpected dishes between the ordered courses.

This is my first experience in eating food that looks more like art. My main dish is a beef bourguignon, and Adam's is a seafood en papillote. We're stuffed after the breads, salads, cheeses, pastas, and our main dishes.

Our walk back to the hotel is refreshing. It feels like we're simultaneously in two worlds, the ancient moat and walls of the Forbidden City on one side and our modern hotel on the other.

The shower in our bathroom is double-sized with two large rain-style showerheads and multiple body-level nozzles. What starts as a joke about saving water and showering together turns into an afternoon of lovemaking.

By this point, I feel so comfortable with Adam that his touch and the feel of his body are as comforting as they are passionate. My experience prior to him was limited. He has enjoyed being my teacher. Now, I learn what turns him on, what drives him crazy, and what can be his undoing.

Ever my explorer, the first man, he unlocks secrets of my body I did not know existed. In his presence and under his eyes, I am all woman, the apex of everything he desires. Confidence can be a fluid thing.

The next morning, Adam posts a couple of pictures from our day before to Twitter. Almost instantly, one receives a reply. That's not uncommon. He has friends and followers remarking on the pictures he posts all the time. However, this virtual friend, a Russian model named Katya, happens to also be in Beijing and would love to hook up—her words, not mine.

We're getting ready to head out the door to go visit the Great Wall, so he direct messages her to meet him—his words, not mine—at the rooftop restaurant of the hotel that night.

When he isn't looking, I sneak a peek at her profile pic. She's tall, has blonde hair down to her ass, and an amazing body. In a word, she's gorgeous.

These ugly seeds of doubt began to worm their way into my head. I'm no longer this unstoppable love goddess. I'm now short, pale, gangly, and unstylish. I pout at my reflection in the mirror, wishing my hair were longer or my cheekbones were more pronounced.

He comes up beside me to brush his teeth. He's in a good mood, excited about meeting a virtual friend in real life. I grab my toothbrush and put on my best happy face, my mind a chaos of what-ifs. I know Adam doesn't want a relationship. It was the first thing he said to me the night of our first kiss. What if he's attracted to her?

I go to the wooden box that holds Ally's ashes and begin carefully pouring some into the smaller plastic box that fits in my cross-body bag. I feel kind of ashamed, like I'm missing the bigger picture. I need to remain focused on what this trip is about, and as much fun as Adam is, I need to make sure I don't lose myself in him. He's temporary. This Eden we've created will end the day the trip does, if not sooner.

I turn. I didn't realize he was watching me.

"Can I look?" he asks, motioning toward the still open box. "I've never seen…" His voice trails off.

"Of course," I reply.

He walks over slowly, almost nervous to disturb the air. He doesn't pick up the box. He just peers into it and tilts it, so some of the ashes inside shift.

"It's strange to think this is what's left of what once was..." I pause, gently pressing the lid shut. "My best friend."

He puts his arm around my shoulders, and he pulls me to him and holds me.

I don't cry every time I think about her, like I did in the beginning. It doesn't mean that I miss her any less now than I did then. It's just that the shock of the pain has dulled over time.

It was the worst when things were brand new with Adam. She would have been the person I confided in. I suppose there's still my mom, but that's different. It hurts that I won't get to tell Ally all about him.

EIGHTEEN

Because of all the walking we did the day before, we decide against walking over to the train station to the Great Wall even though our guidebook says it's only a twenty-minute walk. Even after all of the planning we did, it takes us twice as long as we expect to actually get onto the wall. A train ride, a bus ride, a short walk that takes forever because of how crowded it is. The ticket line to get to the wall, then the choice between waiting and paying for the cable car ride up or taking the steps.

Even though there's a wait for the cable car, I talk Adam into skipping the steps. I'm already done with the wall, and I haven't even stepped one foot onto it.

"Are we there yet?" There's no withholding the whine from my tone.

The nonstop traveling is taking its toll on me. We should have scheduled more down days to recover. Our assumption that we could rest on the long flights was foolish. It's impossible to get comfortable in the seats, and even with headphones on, there's always some sort of distraction to keep us from really sleeping.

He takes a deep breath, like he's willing himself to be calm with me. "I know it has been an ordeal getting here, but once we get in the cable car, our next stop will be the wall."

I feel awful for annoying Adam. I do. It's just that the whole process of getting to where we're at that moment sucks, and I'm not handling it as well as he is.

We're visiting the Badaling area of the wall because it's the closest to Beijing. That's probably the same reason everyone else is. Once we're on the wall, to give each other some space, Adam goes to one side, and I go to the other. My annoyance evaporates with minutes of actually being on the wall.

I find Adam, and we start walking away from the crowds. Thank God we're both wearing sneakers with good traction. The pathway of the wall isn't always level. There are plenty of stairs, some steeper than others, but the slick spots are in these smooth pitched inclines. It rains almost every afternoon in the summer, and the stones aren't always dried out from the day before. I pity anyone around us in flip-flops.

It takes some time and more stairs than I ever want to climb, but we find ourselves almost alone on the Great Wall of China. Our expressions mirror each other's, like, *Holy shit, this is really cool.*

Adam actually smiles. He fists the front of my T-shirt and pulls me to him, planting his lips on mine. It's excitement, enthusiasm, and pure joy in sharing this experience together. We break our kiss and look in either direction to see this never-ending wall, this wonder of the world.

Sobering up a bit, Adam tucks a strand of my wind-tussled hair behind my ear. "Would you like to be alone when you..." He lets the shrug of his shoulder finish his question.

He wants to give me space to be with Ally. I rest my hands on his shoulders, lifting up onto my toes to dust my lips across his, before nodding. He takes his camera and goes to take pictures, giving me some time to myself.

I look out over the greenery, the sloping mountainside full of dips and valleys, and I hold the small plastic box. I consciously let my mind fill itself with Ally. I have a picture show ready on demand. Her kind eyes, her smile, even how she kind of always smelled like vanilla.

With each stop, as I leave a piece of her behind, the pretty wooden box she rests in gets lighter. With each stop, I am leaving a piece of myself with her in my grief. I pause my internal reflection as a small group passes me.

Life is like that. One moment, you can feel like the only person in the world, and the next, you're suddenly within a sea of people.

As quickly as they come, they continue on, and I'm alone again. This isn't like the other times where I placed her ashes on the ground. This time, I reach my arm out as far as I can through one of the openings in the wall, and I just let her go.

She doesn't just crash down to the ground far, far below. The wind catches her, and for a brief moment, she seems suspended in midair before she's gone. She will become part of this place. The rain will come later in the day to dissolve her into the earth.

It gives me peace, knowing that would have made her happy. I can imagine her thinking of all the schoolchildren who come here on field trips. It's a place of wonder and possibilities.

Adam stands a ways off, leaning against the opening of a watchtower. I motion for him to come over to me, and he does.

He drapes his arm around my shoulders and kisses the side of my head, which is strangely comforting. "You okay?"

I nod, slipping my hand into his. We stay in that spot a few more moments. Adam takes a picture of a bird in flight, and then suddenly, an entire flock takes flight before us. If he hadn't already had his camera ready, he would have missed it.

Once they're out of sight, he turns to look at me, eyes wide. "Whoa."

I laugh. "That was awesome."

He peers down at his camera, scratching the back of his head in almost disbelief.

We slowly make our way back down to the cable car. He wisely bought some snacks from the hotel gift shop before we left that morning. We eat as we sit on a bench, waiting for the train to take us back to Beijing. Even though I wore comfortable shoes, my feet throb from the two hours we spent walking the wall.

It starts raining right after we board. On the train, I sleep, sagging with my head on Adam's shoulder. He shakes me awake when we reach our stop, and then he pulls me back against him for the cab ride back to the hotel.

He laughs as I collapse onto our bed once we're back at the hotel. I can't help it. My legs tremble like Jell-O. After stepping out of his sneakers and tugging mine off of me, he joins me.

We still have to meet Katya for dinner. His phone wakes us a couple of hours later. I groan as he reaches over me to silence it. When he chuckles, I peer at him through a curtain of my hair.

"What?" I mumble, not awake enough to fully form my consonants.

"You"—he pushes my hair to the side—"are not a morning person."

"It's not morning," I argue, covering my face with a pillow.

The weight on the bed shifts, and he's straddling me. I have another moment of blissful darkness before he lifts the pillow off of my head.

"We still need to get ready for dinner. Want to share a shower?" He raises one brow, his hands slipping under my shirt.

"Won't we be late?" I ask, not really caring and feeling more awake.

In the shower, he moves with urgency, fully focused on our mutual release. I'm pliable and mold into the object of his desire. I can see it burning in his eyes, his want for me. I'm a person I don't know when I'm in his arms. I'm confident and aggressive. I need to learn to hold on to some of that outside of him.

Despite our rushed lovemaking, we're still late for dinner. I was hoping I could devote an extra five minutes to making myself look presentable. As usual, I'm wearing a wrinkled dress, and I finger comb my damp hair in the elevator.

Before the doors open, Adam asks a question that somehow sucks any confidence I gained from me. "Are you sure you want to come?"

My mouth drops before I can think. I close my mouth. "Do you not want me to come?"

He hesitates, watching the doors open. Neither of us moves.

"I don't want you to feel bored."

I tilt my head at him, hearing the doors close. "Why would I be bored?"

"Never mind," he murmurs, pressing the button for the roof again.

When we walk out, he doesn't reach for my hand. I've become accustomed to him doing it, so it stings when he doesn't. He makes a beeline for the bar as I follow three steps behind, trying to keep up. It reminds me of him losing me in the airport on our first day together.

Next thing I know, he's shaking her hand, introducing her to the void he assumes is me as I walk up. His eyes widen briefly as I extend my hand to her and introduce myself. Has he realized what he's done? She takes her drink off the bar top and carries it with her as we're seated. Her English is great, her accent charming.

I watch as they laugh over inside jokes having to do with Twitter conversations and hashtags. I have no idea what they're talking about.

I use my lack of involvement in the conversation to study her. She has long, almost white blonde hair. It's pulled back in a long ponytail and swung over one shoulder, hanging down to cover her breast. I wonder if it's all her own hair or if she has extensions. Before my hair envy overpowers me, I watch her face, her expressions, as she speaks to Adam.

She has an easy smile. I'm relieved that Adam, while seemingly happy, does not smile back. You have to earn those smiles. She has toothpaste commercial–ready teeth. I absentmindedly run my tongue across mine, wondering if they're as white as hers.

Her complexion is probably naturally fair, like mine, but she wears a healthy golden tan. She also wears a white sleeveless sheath dress. It sets off her tan and broadcasts the fact that she probably didn't dribble her food and is brave enough to wear white while traveling.

I don't want to like her. I want her to be an annoying idiot who Adam cannot be mentally attracted to.

But she's lovely, intelligent, engagingly animated, as she shares her travel stories with us. Even when Adam excuses himself from our table and we're alone together, she's warm and seems genuinely interested in learning about me. Her worldliness picks at my internal insecurities. She's been places. Sure, I have as well, but she's gone to them by herself. She has a career and is self-sufficient.

Her success amplifies my inadequacies in my mind. This trip is supposed to be a way for me to gain my independence, maybe even allow me to decide what I want to do with my life.

Katya is working on her master's degree in physiology with plans to pursue her doctorate. She's smart, successful, beautiful, and interesting.

After our meals are cleared, I start to wonder if I'm a third wheel. I excuse myself. I'm nothing but polite, telling her how nice it was to meet her.

Leaning into Adam, I ask for our room key.

As he passes it to me, I tell him, "Just knock, and I'll—"

He stops me. "You don't have to. I brought both room keys just in case."

In case? My eyes flick to his, but he's already turned his back to her.

I finally admit to myself that I was testing him to see if he would come back with me. He failed. I say my good-byes and pout the whole way back to our room. We're leaving China tomorrow and taking a red-eye flight to Australia.

Our trip will be ending soon, and here I am, falling for him. I need to distance myself from him, from what we're doing, before I get hurt any more than I already am.

I have the hardest time falling asleep. I'm used to his presence, his scent, and his arms around me. I finally nod off a couple of hours later.

I awake briefly to his gentle snore, his arm draped over me, before slipping back under. We talked about trying to see the Summer Palace today. His late night and forgetting to set the alarm allows us a lazy morning instead.

I bite my tongue, wanting to ask what time he got in, curious at what happened after I left last night. My jealousy embarrasses me. This, us, is temporary. How together we seemed, our physical camaraderie, was just a side effect of traveling together.

This morning, when he reaches for me, I pull away.

He sits up. "Everything okay?"

I nod, a nonverbal lie, and look away.

"Come here."

He's on to me.

I inch closer to him but stay just out of his grasp. I watch his fingers flex, knowing he wants to touch me. I still want him to. I'm trying to be smart about this. We've already gone too far. I only want to protect myself.

"Just tell me." He shifts closer to me.

I can't meet his eyes, so I stare at my hands instead. "I just think maybe this isn't a good idea."

"Aubrey, look at me." He sounds confused.

My eyes flick to his, and my mouth is suddenly dry. "We're both going to be going our separate ways soon. It seems smart to stop now before either of us gets attached. You can be with other people." I pause. "Like Katya."

He drops his head to rest on his fist, his elbow on his knee, and he just looks at me, like he is trying to figure me out. "What if I don't want to stop? Katya is only a friend."

"But you stayed out with her last night. This"—I motion to the empty void between us—"is only delaying the inevitable," I argue weakly, wondering what I am to him. I don't want to stop either.

He moves, pinning me to the mattress. "Nothing happened with her. Don't you know I only have eyes for you?" He waggles his brows at me. "And we shouldn't waste the time we have together."

"But I'm scared I'll get hurt," I admit, losing myself in his gray eyes.

They darken. "I won't hurt you."

I lift my lips to his in surrender, thinking that he doesn't even know he already has.

Afterward, we make our way to the double shower. Just as I have grown so used to falling asleep with him, I start to wonder if I can shower alone again without missing him. He washes me, his soapy hands gliding over every inch of me. He lets me wash his hair. His hands are on my hips as I face him, hands in his hair.

The first time I saw him, I thought he looked perfect. He isn't though. His ears stick out a bit, and he has a wrinkle between his eyebrows from how often they come together. He has a faint farmer's tan, and he doesn't smile enough. He can be bossy and annoying. He likes doing things his way to a fault, but he's also protective and gentle, even when he's being rough.

He doesn't let me pull away when I try, and I'm in love with him.

We have time to kill between our checkout and needing to be at the airport. We go to the airport and check in, just so we won't have to carry our suitcases around with us, and then we have lunch. There are some half-day tours we think about trying but end up just staying at the airport.

There are five flights leaving from our gate before ours. We find a couple of seats away from the blast of the air conditioning vent and hang out. Adam explores a gift shop at one point while I read. I'm not paying attention and jump when he reaches for my hand. He's taken over finding charms for my bracelet. Today, he gives me two.

"I wasn't sure which you would like more," he says, handing me a small pagoda and a watchtower.

"I love them both," I say truthfully, holding my hand out to him to attach them to my bracelet.

He dips his mouth, dropping a kiss to the inside of my wrist, before letting my hand go.

His sweet gesture unlocks my tongue. "Will you miss me when I'm gone?"

He feigns confusion. "Going somewhere?"

I lean against him, resting my head on his shoulder. "I'll be back in California, and you'll be in New York."

"But we're both here right now."

Can it be that simple? Just living in the moment, no care or worry for what will happen tomorrow?

I let it go and read my book. From his position behind me, he reads along. I don't even know he's doing it until he asks me to turn the page back, that he's still on the last paragraph.

I tilt my face back toward his. "Do you want me to catch you up?"

"Seems to be a lot of sex. I think I'm caught up."

I blush. "It's more than just sex."

He raises a brow. "If you say so. It's cool. It's kinda hot. You want me to tie you up too?"

My mouth drops, but I don't say no.

He licks his lips before dropping his mouth to my ear. "Turn the page. I'm getting ideas."

We read together, pausing only when either of us gets up to grab some food or goes to the restroom and then when our plane starts boarding. Reading a hot book is one thing. Thinking everything that's happening to the main character might happen to you is a whole different experience. I can't remember the last time I finished a book as fast.

Our flight is twelve hours. We're able to sleep at least six each on the plane. When we land and once we're through immigration, we head straight to our hotel. We have connecting rooms overlooking the harbor. Adam ignores his room, dropping his things in mine instead.

We don't have anything planned that day, other than wandering the city and enjoying the views of the harbor. I suggest we have drinks after dinner, but Adam seems in an awful hurry to get back to our room.

It seems he does want to tie me up. Seated in the armchair that faces the bed, he asks that I strip. There's a dresser with a large mirror above it behind him. I watch my own eyes widen. This is turning him on. From where I stand, I can see the bulge in his pants straining against the fabric. I step out of my flats, pushing them with one foot away from the bed. I have a gray cardigan on. I slide it off one shoulder and then the other, and I let it fall to the floor behind me.

I unbutton my jeans, and then I slowly slide the zipper down. I turn, so my back is to him, and I bend at the waist as I ease them down my legs. I glance back at him and see him breathing heavily and shifting in his seat.

I step out of my jeans and turn back to him as I start unbuttoning my shirt. I'm teasing him, going slowly from one button to the next. After I free the final button, I let my shirt hang open for a moment and look at him again.

"Off," he commands, his tone raising the tiny hairs on the back of my neck.

I peel the shirt from my body and let it fall on top of my jeans. I start to reach to unclasp my simple white bra, but he gets up and strides over to me. He takes my hands and places them on his chest. I can feel the thump of his heart beneath his

T-shirt. He slips one of my bra straps down, trailing its descent down my shoulder with his lips.

I lean into him, my legs tingling. He repeats the motion and the trail of kisses on my other shoulder before spinning me so that my back is to him. He releases the back clasp, and my bra falls to the floor in front of me.

I sag against his chest. His hands reach around to cup and toy with my breasts. Turning me again, he claims my lips, his hands now in my hair. My hands move to slip under his shirt. I want the weight of his chest pressed against mine.

"Easy," he murmurs onto my lips.

He eases me onto the bed. I scoot back toward the pillows and watch him, mouth open, as he pulls off his shirt. His body is a thing of beauty. The tone of his chest, the definition of his abs and arms. I love touching him. Even now, my fingers itch to explore him.

His eyes are locked on mine as he slowly slips his belt off. He doesn't drop it to the floor like he did his shirt. He holds it in his hand, his jeans now sagging in a way that makes my mouth water, as he makes his way over to me.

I watch, almost detached, as he binds my hands together and then secures the belt to the headboard.

"But I like touching you," I argue even though I'm excited.

He lies between my legs, holding himself up over me. "I know you do."

He lowers his lips to my rib cage. It makes me think of him as the first man again, inspecting his stolen rib through my skin. His mouth moves lower to tease the hem of my underwear. It's funny to think the quick-dry ones my mother ordered from a catalog turn him on as much as they do. Maybe it's because the material is so thin. He kisses me through them, burying his face between my thighs. It's amazing but not enough. He's teasing me.

I don't want that strip of material between us. I want his lips on my skin. I buck my hips against him, groaning in protest. If my hands were free, I could just take off my own underwear, but I'm at his mercy. He can toy with me as long as he wants.

I know he's turned on though, so I plead, "Please, Adam. God, I want you so bad right now."

He looks up at me, tilting his head to the side, his fingers stroking the skin above my underwear. "But you wanted to stop."

I can't believe he's bringing that up. "I don't want to stop."

"Are you sure? Because if you do…" His voice trails off.

My body is practically humming with want. I throw my head back and squeeze my eyes shut. The way he turns my words against me, reminding me that I tried to stop us, stings. I don't understand why the idea of us going our separate ways is already killing me. Bound, unable to touch him, knowing soon I'll never be able to touch him, is too much for me.

He knows something is wrong. He crawls up my body and sees my eyes pinched shut. He frees my hands from his belt before pulling me into his arms.

"I wasn't trying to upset you," he whispers before kissing me.

My hands drown in the feel of him, roaming shamelessly over his shoulders and down his back. "I just need to touch you right now."

"Okay," he murmurs, pushing me onto my back.

His earlier patience is lost. He attacks me, and I'm overwhelmed by the pleasure in my surrender. His lips search for mine as he fills me. We cling to each other, spent.

"I was supposed to be watching my cousin."

I look up at him and see rain clouds in his eyes. I don't say anything. I just let him keep speaking.

"I was seventeen, and my uncle's house was on the river. There was a place where we used to swim but always with one of our parents watching."

He drops his head to my shoulder and takes a shaky breath. "I had just turned seventeen, so they thought I was old enough to watch the younger ones. There were five of us out there that day. I was helping one of them out of the water when she went under. I hadn't seen her swim that far from the dock. The river was high, the current a lot faster than normal. My cousin, Mandy, got stuck in it. I tried to reach her, swim after her, but I was so slow. I couldn't get to her in time. She was ten."

I pull him closer, wrapping my arms around him.

"I lost the weight after that."

"It wasn't your fault," I whisper.

He lifts his head, his eyes haunted. "I know that now. It's just...I was supposed to be watching them."

I kiss him, and we hold each other. I run my fingers through his hair, reeling at his confession. I do the math in my head, realizing that the cousin who died was born the same year own his mother had died. What a horrible, tragic coincidence.

NINETEEN

We're up early the next morning for our excursion, a guided day tour. Neither of us mentions his confession from the night before. I don't know what to say to him.

Our pickup for the bus is near our hotel. We sit together near the middle and watch as the bus fills up at each stop. Our first stop is a hands-on wildlife park an hour outside of Sydney.

I've always been an animal lover, so I'm in heaven. The animals in the section of the park we're in are tame. It's an exotic petting zoo. Adam is in full-on paparazzi mode as he takes my picture with all of them.

A young koala steals my heart as he clings to my chest. One of the guides explains this koala is nicknamed Sparky. He was displaced from his natural habitat by a wildfire. He's here in this park to be rehabilitated and hopefully released into the wild.

We explore one enclosure after another to see animals native to Australia. There's one interactive enclosure where we get to feed kangaroos. For some reason, they prefer me over Adam. They make him so nervous that he takes most of his pictures of them from outside their enclosure.

The park gives each of us a souvenir, a small stuffed koala or kangaroo, on the way out of the park. We both get kangaroos and Adam gives his to me.

From the park, our group goes to lunch near Leura. After lunch, we have time to wander the town, which has a healthy number of tourist shops. I am with Adam when he asks me to pick out the next charm for my bracelet. I can't decide between the Sydney Opera House, a boomerang, or a bear. I finally settle on the boomerang just because of the way it was painted, and it would add some color to my wrist. Adam gets me a bear as well, so I can remember Sparky.

We travel to the Three Sisters next, possibly the most famous landmark within the Blue Mountains. Three rocky peaks, standing side by side. The legend behind the sisters is sad. There were three sisters—Meehni, Wimlah, and Gunnedoo. They lived many years ago in the Jamison Valley and were members of the Katoomba tribe.

They were beautiful and had many suitors, but they fell in love with three brothers from the Nepean tribe. Tribal law forbid their marriages, and the brothers, angry, decided to kidnap the sisters to force the marriages.

A giant battle broke out between the two tribes, and in an effort to protect the sisters, a witch doctor turned them to stone. His intentions were good. He had planned to turn them back once the battle was over and they were safe. Instead, the witch doctor was killed during the battle, and there was no one else who could reverse his spell. So, they stand to this day, frozen in stone for all time.

Our tour takes us to a place called Echo Point. There's a platform there, overlooking the Three Sisters and the valley. I move away from the rest of the tour to the edge of the platform, not closest to the sisters and everyone taking pictures.

The three sisters remind me of the relationship I had with my mother and Ally. Ally wasn't truly my sister, but it felt like she was. She acted in so many ways as the bridge between my mother and me. I can see her represented in the rock, holding my mother and me together.

I sit down and cross my legs, holding the small plastic box. I speak to her, tell her what Adam shared with me the night before. I wish she could have been there to tell me what to do. I miss her guidance. I tip the box over the edge of the platform, letting her ashes fall into the valley below.

That morning, when I poured some ashes from the wooden carved box into my smaller plastic box that fit in my purse, I was shocked at how little was left. I only have two more places where I plan to release her ashes. The thought of that, the end of my good-bye trip with her, scares me.

Adam hangs back, knowing I need my space. When I'm finished, I go to find him. He's taking pictures of the joints of the railing that enclose the overlook platform. I'm sure he also took pictures of the sisters, but I love that it's still the way things come together that most interest him.

We ride a yellow cable car next to get a closer look at the sisters and the valley below. The floor is made of glass, and it's like we're floating over the rainforest. The height makes me nervous. I think I would have felt more comfortable sitting than standing. I use Adam for support, wrapping my arms around his waist. My cheek is to his back as he takes pictures of our journey.

A railway car pulls us backward and brings us back to where we started. The railcar also has a glass ceiling. We sit and look skyward at the full green-limbed branches above us. There are white birds, maybe a type of parrot, with a yellow crest that remains undisturbed by our skyward jaunt. The sensation of being pulled backward and not seeing where we're going does not agree with my stomach.

I'm thankful I didn't get sick from the motion by the time the ride is over. Walking around with my feet on solid ground helps the feeling pass before we get back onto the bus.

From there, we head to the Parramatta River. We'll take a cruise back to the Circular Quay of the Sydney Harbor and be back where we started. The boat is crowded but not overly so.

We sit on the top deck. I pull a hair tie out of my purse and make a feeble attempt at pulling my hair back. It's grown a bit on the trip but still isn't long enough to hold in a ponytail. I settle by pulling it half up. My hair still whirls in the wind but now mostly off my face.

There's a British family we haven't met before also on our tour. Their teenage daughter seems taken with Adam. I smile quietly as she asks him questions about his camera and the States.

"Do you have a car?" She bats her eyelashes at him.

He inches closer to me on our seat. "Where I live, you don't need one."

I slip my arm through his and bite back a smile at her annoyed expression. She finally gives up and leaves to chat up some Australian boys a few rows away.

"Were you ever like that?"

I think back to when I was in high school before Ally got sick. "I had a boyfriend for most of my senior year, but I was a bit of a flirt. I don't think I ever hit on an older guy though."

He looks offended. "Older?"

"I'm not saying you're old." I laugh as his expression of mock horror relaxes. "But to her. You might be almost twice her age."

"So, if she comes back, I should mention my retirement savings to scare her away?"

"See, I don't even have that."

"No 401(k)? I only have one because my company matches my contribution."

I look out over the water. "I don't even have a job."

He slips his arm around me, pulling me closer. "So, my spoiled comment wasn't that far off?"

I do my best to look offended. "I might be unemployed, but I don't think I'm spoiled."

He pretends to think about it for a moment. "I guess not."

"I'm not sure what to do once this trip is over. Do I go back to school or just get a job and move out? I was hoping I would have had some sort of epiphany on what to do with my life by now."

"I still don't know," he admits.

"You seem to have it together though. You have a job and an apartment, you travel, you..." I wrinkle my nose, trying to think of more things. "Tweet?"

His brows come together at my last comment, and he shakes his head. "I have a boring job that I stay at to pay the bills. I have possibly the smallest apartment in the city. I'm not even going to touch your tweet comment."

"What would you rather be doing?"

He shrugs. "I don't know. I guess I'm just treading water until I figure it out."

"Are you...do you ever talk to your dad?"

He inhales sharply. "Not that much. We email more than anything else. He likes me to send pictures from my trips."

We're both quiet the rest of the cruise, the bus ride to the drop-off spot, and then the walk back to the hotel.

I use his laptop to check my email.

"Conner can drive up tomorrow," I tell him, looking up from the screen.

"Great." He sounds annoyed.

"Don't be like that," I grumble, knowing he isn't thrilled to see my partner in bungee-jumping crime again.

He lifts his hands innocently. "Like what?"

I set the laptop on the table next to me and walk over to him, wrapping my arms around his waist. "Conner is just a friend. Don't be grumpy."

He leans down to kiss my forehead. "No jumping off of bridges. Deal?"

I pop up onto my toes and kiss him. "Deal."

Wiped from the day and the days before, we order room service for dinner. We then share a bath, now somewhat revived from dinner. There's a deep circular tub in the bathroom that overlooks the harbor. I sit in his lap, my back to his chest, as we watch the ships pass by.

We lose interest in our view when his lips move to my neck. Water laps over the edge of the tub and onto the floor as we move together. Any secrets my body held from him in the beginning, he long ago unlocked. He knows where and how to touch me to bring me the most pleasure.

Conner drives up from his home in Wollongong to meet us at our hotel. We check out and load our bags into his car. His eyes widen when he sees my hand in Adam's, but he doesn't say anything.

I sit up front with Conner. We drive to Bondi Beach. It's close to Sydney, so Conner can have us back in plenty of time for our flight that night. He tells us all about the rest of his trip with his family, and I tell him all we've seen. He seems really interested in going to India. He's trying to talk his folks into that being their trip next year.

He parks and looks over at me. "Pity it isn't warmer. This beach is topless."

I cross my arms over my chest and avoid Adam's eyes, knowing he's probably pissed. Once we're all out of the car, he reaches for my hand. I look up at him then, and yep, he's glaring at Conner. This should be fun.

We eat at a Japanese place for lunch before walking out onto the beach. Despite the chill, there are surfers in wetsuits catching waves. I carry my sandals in my hand and lift my long maxi skirt to keep it from getting wet. The water isn't warm, and I back away quickly. Adam looks at me, curious.

I shrug. "I've grown up within driving distance of this ocean my whole life. Now, I've seen it and felt it from both sides."

We do the cliff walk from Bondi to Coogee. We stop in Bronte for a smoothie and watch the surfers. The water is beautiful, almost mint-colored from our vantage point. It's nice to focus on that instead of Conner and Adam trying to one-up each other. When we were in Africa, the vibe I got from Conner was almost brotherly. Here, he's definitely flirting with me.

When we get back to Bondi and Adam is out of hearing range, I call Conner out on it. "Why are you acting like this?"

He glances around, making sure Adam isn't near us. "Just having some fun, driving your fella mad."

I smack his arm and point at him. "Stop it. I'm stuck on a plane with him tonight."

He drapes his arm around my shoulders in a move I know will piss Adam off and hugs me to him. It's pointless. He's having too much fun.

Adam doesn't look happy when he walks up to us moments later.

Conner grins. "If I'm ever in California, will you be my tour guide?"

I slip out from under his arm and put some distance between us. "Of course."

Adam is quiet during the trip to the airport.

As Conner pulls away from the curb, Adam turns to me. "Still don't like that kid."

"He's not that bad," I argue, following Adam into the terminal.

We're flying to Argentina. From there, we have a connecting flight to Rio de Janeiro. By tomorrow evening, we'll be back in the Americas, one stop closer to our trip being over.

I'm trying to keep what Adam said in my mind, that we're together now, but I can't stop thinking about when we'll have to say good-bye. I'm obsessing over it. That, and the fact that we'll be staying with a friend of my mom's. I'm dreading the sleep-arrangement conversation. There will be no way to disguise we're something more than just travel companions.

Constance and my mom were college roommates. Constance moved back to Brazil after getting her degree. She and her husband, Raul, never had children. I've never met her, and I can only hope she's cool. South America has a large Catholic population. I'm worried about her opinion on premarital sex.

"Worst case, we can always get a hotel," Adam reminds me once we're seated on the plane.

"Part of the reason my parents were cool with me even going to Brazil is because we'd be with someone who lives there."

We've both seen the news. Brazil, Rio in particular, does not have a reputation for being the safest place. At least Constance lives in Leblon, a safe, high-end neighborhood.

I have a hard time sleeping on the plane. There's a toddler a few rows behind us who cries off and on for long portions of the flight. I pity the parents while I wish the little one would just go to sleep.

Adam sleeps straight through. I eventually find a documentary in which the narrator's monotone voice lulls me to sleep. However, I'm still exhausted by the time we land in Argentina.

Not caring that I take up an extra seat at our next gate, I lie down with my head in Adam's lap. We have a three-hour layover before our flight to Rio. I sleep through most of it and can still hardly keep my eyes open once we board.

Our flight to Rio isn't long but going through immigration is. It's over an hour before we make our way to baggage claim.

"Aubrey?"

I turn to see a slim dark-haired woman behind me. "Mrs. Alberto?"

"Please, call me Constance," she says, opening her arms to hug me.

I introduce her to Adam. We wait together for our luggage and then follow her to the parking area. She drives a high-end compact car. Adam loads our bags in the trunk, and at my insistence, he sits up front to have more legroom.

With traffic, it takes some time to get to her apartment. Constance points out landmarks along the way. She parks in an underground lot beneath her building. Her apartment is on the ninth out of twelve floors. It's light and airy with big floor-to-ceiling windows in the main living and dining areas.

"Your rooms are this way."

We follow her down a hallway, and when we get to the rooms, I clear my throat.

"Would it be all right if we shared a room?" I ask, my face getting red.

She looks at Adam and then back at me. "Does your mama know about this?"

I slowly shake my head.

She takes a deep breath. "You are both adults. I appreciate you being upfront and asking. Of course you may share a room." She pauses. "The blue room has a bigger bed."

Adam moves our bags into the blue room. Thankfully, the master bedroom is on the other side of the apartment.

Adam and I shower separately and change into fresh clothes before meeting her in the living room.

It's strange being observed. If we had been in a hotel, we might have made love already and ordered room service. Instead, she has a tray prepared with sliced meat, cheese, and crackers. We snack and hang out on the balcony until Mr. Alberto, Raul, comes home from work.

Constance wants to hear about our trip. She has Adam power up his laptop, so she can see all of the pictures he's taken so far. Once Raul retires, they plan to travel the world.

"Don't wait. Go now while you can," I burst, out of nowhere.

She looks at me, eyes wide. When it hits her, she puts her hand on my arm. "I'm so sorry for your loss, *querida*."

That night we go to Platforma, a place where we have dinner and then watch a carnival-style samba performance. The costumes are incredible, and while some of the dancers give lackluster performances, the show overall is a lot of fun.

As we walk back to their apartment, Raul goes on about Carnival. "Sure, getting around town is miserable during the carnival, but this is Rio, and you must come back sometime to experience it. There is nothing like it."

Constance rolls her eyes at his exuberance but agrees that if we ever want to see the real carnival, we're welcome to stay with them.

"Thanks. Might take a break from traveling for a bit after this trip though," I admit.

Sinking into Adam's waiting arms is the best part of my day. I'm tired of traveling, tired of seeing new places. As much as I don't want the trip to end, I crave normalcy. Adam has become that for me—my constant. He folds me into his arms in yet another new bed. We don't make love that night. Sleep takes us away before anything can happen.

I awake to his lips on my skin the next morning. He's making up for lost time, wanting to taste me before he has to share me.

We're comfortable lovers by now, our rhythm down. My hips rise to meet his in our choreographed coupling. We're quiet, and he's gentle.

I'm in love with him. I wonder how he feels about me, but I'm too scared to ask. I don't want to ruin our last days together.

I leave him in bed as I go shower. When I come back into our room, he pulls me back into bed and licks stray beads of water from my neck and shoulders.

We freeze when Constance knocks on our bedroom door. "Do either of you drink coffee?"

I cover myself even though I know she can't see me through the door. "Coffee would be great. Thanks."

After another lingering kiss, he takes his shower while I get dressed. I don't wait for him, and I join Constance on the balcony. He is there, with us not long after.

That day, we go to Corcovado to see the Christ Statue. It's crowded, but the views of the city below are amazing. We have lunch in the city afterward.

"And how is your mother?"

I have to think for a moment. It's been so long since I've seen her. "She started volunteering at an animal shelter. It makes her happy and gives her something to do."

"Your aunt." She shakes her head. "It was such a shame."

"It was," I agree.

Adam reaches under the table to hold my hand, his thumb moving back and forth across the top of it. His simple gesture pierces my careful mask. I don't break down, but I have to blink away tears that were not there a moment ago.

After lunch, we make our way to Sugar Loaf Mountain. There's a cable car that takes us to the top. My mother told Constance that I would have some of Ally's ashes with me to spread. It was my mom's idea to do it here. I can't decide which view is better, Corcovado or Sugar Loaf.

What is nice about Sugar Loaf is that there's more room to move around and explore. There's even a small gift shop where Adam finds another charm for my bracelet. As I wander off, trying to find the perfect place, I come across a couple of small monkeys.

I don't approach them. I just stand still and watch them as one climbs up on a post and looks back at me. He's a furry little guy with dark hair all over, except for the white tufts of hair at his ears. If I wasn't so scared that he'd probably bite me, I might try to get closer to him. Given the amount of people that visit each year, I wonder how tame the monkeys are.

I take his appearance as a sign of where Ally should rest. Up this high, there isn't a bad view, and somehow, the fact that the little monkey watches me spread her ashes comforts me. It makes me feel like I'm not leaving her alone, that maybe he'll continue to watch over her.

I'm more emotional than I have been the last few times I spread her ashes because I know I'll be finished soon. I'm not ready to really say good-bye to her.

When we get back to the Albertos' apartment, we do laundry, and when Raul gets home from work, we walk to a local restaurant. I've started trying different foods along the way with Adam. I still have a fairly bland palate in comparison to him, but when I like something that I didn't think I would, he smiles every time.

It's late when we get back to the apartment. We didn't eat dinner until nine that night. Adam and I aren't tired though. We stay up, later than we should, enjoying each other.

I wore a short dress tonight. Adam doesn't even bother getting me out of it once we're alone in our room. He simply pushes himself inside me. His impatience makes me feel powerful.

I know he wants me and is turned on by my nakedness. It thrills me that even covered up, he has to have me. He's frantic in the way he takes me. Normally, I can match his tempo, but tonight, I just hold on to him. It's fast and hard and thrilling, but when he finds his release, my body is still moments away from mine. He knows.

Afterward, he slowly undresses me and makes up for that, over and over. Just when I think I can't take it anymore, he pushes inside me once more. His earlier attention leaves my flesh primed. I'm lost in an ocean of him. When the waves crash over me, more powerful this time than any previous, I drag him under with me.

He props himself over me with his arms, and we stare at each other. He sinks down onto me, turning me, so we're on our sides, facing each other.

He reaches up to brush some hair off my face, his hand coming back to hold my cheek. "What are you doing to me?"

It's more a statement than a question.

Even though it's winter in Brazil, it's still warm enough to go to the beach the next day. Constance takes us to Ipanema Beach. This is the first time Adam sees me in a bikini. He smooths sunblock over my skin. I thrill in returning the favor, seeing the looks other beachgoers give him. We lay out for most of the afternoon.

We return to the apartment to shower before our flight. Constance is more sentimental at my leaving than I expected. I can see she misses my mother. Now that my father is easing into retirement and once I'm home, I can talk my parents into visiting Rio themselves.

Adam and I have another long evening flight. The sun wore me out, so I don't have a problem sleeping on this flight. We fly to Miami. It's odd to be in the States again. This is our stopover as there were no direct flights to the island.

We land at midday in St. Martin. A car takes us to the resort. Again, we have rooms with a connecting door. After we started sharing a bed, Adam wanted to cancel the extra rooms for the rest of the trip. I stopped him. It's silly, but I don't want my parents finding out that way. Since all the travel arrangements are on my dad's credit card, it's better to say nothing.

The walls are white, and golden brown furniture with rattan inserts fill the room. I step out of my shoes and onto the cool blue tiled floor. The tiles match the bedding and accents.

As pretty as the room is, it's the view that captivates me. A sliding double door leads out to a small patio with privacy walls on each side. The ocean is right there, just steps from the patio. I open the door and move out onto it, the ocean breeze on my face. Adam follows, standing behind me, his arms around my waist.

It's good to be on our own again. We change into our suits and go straight to the beach. The ocean water is warm but still refreshing. In Brazil, we did nothing more than get our feet wet. Here, we swim. We play like children, splashing and dunking each other. We're soon exhausted. We rinse off in the outdoor shower before napping away most of the afternoon.

I surprise Adam that night by ordering a buttered tilapia for dinner. He says nothing but watches me intently as I take my first bite. I know he's waiting for a reaction, something to let him know if I like it or not.

I lift my napkin, daintily dabbing the corners of my mouth, before dropping it back in my lap and leaning toward him. "Absolutely delicious."

He bites into his king-sized shrimp with gusto. "Alfredo next."

I wrinkle my nose at the thought, and he laughs.

"First girl who's ever turned down my alfredo," he jokes, raising one brow.

"It's not like you made it. It was takeout," I argue.

"Interesting. Would you have eaten some if I'd made it?"

I shake my head and take another bite.

After dinner, we share an ice cream sundae. Adam holds the cherry out for me. I keep my eyes on him as I close my lips around it. His breath hitches as he watches me.

That night, we make love with the patio door open, our bodies matching the break of the waves hitting the shore. It's after midnight and already our last full day together. I hope the darkness of our room hides the tears slipping from my eyes.

I awake before Adam the next morning. I don't need the small plastic box this time. I cradle the beautifully carved wooden box that holds my best friend and go outside. I sit with her in the sand. My legs are crossed. Her box sits on my lap.

I watch the sunrise bleed orange into the ocean as it slowly makes its ascent. The void within me, left by her passing, hits me all over again. She wanted me to take this journey, so I could grow and find out who I am. The only things I'm sure of are that I miss her more now than I did when I started, and I know tomorrow I'll say good-bye to the man I love.

I press the box to my chest, its corners digging into me. It's not designed to be held. It's made to hold something. I sob as I open the lid. I blink and peer into the box, not believing she's almost gone.

Before I can talk myself out of it and hold on to her a bit longer, I tilt the box and spill her ashes in the sand in front of me. Her ashes mix right into the white sand so quickly that I flex my fingers in the spot. It's as if I've lost her all over again.

I pull my knees to my chest, drop my head, and cry. I startle when strong arms wrap around me. Adam must have woken up to find me gone, and he went off in search of me. He didn't need to go far. I'm steps away from our patio. He holds me as I mourn Ally.

"Shh, I'm here," he says, holding me tightly.

He picks me and the box up and carries me back to our room, setting the now empty box on the table beside me. He closes the sliding door to the patio and pulls the shades, darkening the room before coming back to our bed. Then, he just holds me.

I mourn the presence of Ally in my life. I mourn the fact that she never had a child of her own. I mourn the wedding she never had. I mourn the trip she didn't get to take, and I mourn not being able to talk to her about Adam.

When I'm finally cried out, Adam dries my face. I reach out for him. I am empty. I need him to fill me. His touch reawakens me and pulls me past my grief.

We don't stray far from our room that day. The only things in our world are the sand, the sun, the surf, and each other. We're saying good-bye tomorrow.

Time doesn't slow for us. The purples and blues of the sun's descent fill the sky. It's our last night together, and I still don't even know if he's going to miss me when I'm gone. I know I'll miss him. I try not to think about it. I can't imagine a day without him in it.

We're quiet over dinner. While the guests around us party, we hardly eat. He stretches his arm across the table, reaching for my hand, like he's trying to get as much of my touch while he still can.

After dinner, we slowly walk back to our room. The beach is lit up by the resort. Somehow, the black of the sky is a shade lighter than the darkness of the ocean, allowing me to differentiate between them. I try to focus on anything other than the fact that this is our last night together. Adam's different too, tense. He fills the night with random words, almost as if the silence scares him.

I listen, dazed, as he speaks about some of his previous trips. After an hour, I tug him inside, realizing what he's doing. He's delaying our going to bed. He's using his stories to stay awake to avoid the night ending. As much as I love hearing about his travels, I kiss him to silence him.

I want to stay awake, feeling his heart beating against mine. I need to lose myself in him again. When my lips touch his, he knows.

Tonight, I shake in his arms and wait for him to tell me how he feels about me. I wait all night for words that never come.

We have the same flight back to the States, stopping in Miami. From there, Adam will fly to New York, and I will go to California.

We make love one last time that morning. I should tell him that I love him right then, but I'm scared that he doesn't love me back. As long as I don't know, I can always hope that he does.

From the hotel to the airport, he only lets go of my hand once to go to the gift shop. Our plane to Miami is small, two seats on one side and only one seat on the other side of the aisle.

I have the window seat. I blink away the tears I don't want him to see as I watch the island disappear from view. Our flight is three hours. He pushes the armrest between us up, and we hold each other the whole flight. I want to memorize his scent, the texture of his fingertips, and the curve of his lips.

Our connecting flights are in different directions. We stand at the halfway point, his hand on my cheek, as he kisses me good-bye.

People bustle all around us, but I only see Adam. I know I'll lose it at my gate, but I hold it together, not wanting him to see me cry.

His flight is leaving an hour after mine. When my flight is boarding, he presses a bag into my hands. I start to open it, but he stops me, telling me to wait until I'm on my plane. He presses one last hard kiss against my lips, and then he leaves. I watch until his figure is swallowed up by the mass of moving souls.

I sleepwalk to my gate, clutching the bag he gave me. I think of Ally and how my falling for Adam clouded what she wanted this trip to be for me. I know right then that I'm going back to school. As scared as I am to live away from home, I know I need to do that too.

I avoid thinking about Adam as I figure out the next steps I will take with my life. I need to move out even if I just rent a room. I'll have to get a job first. Maybe I can temp or waitress. These thoughts help me hold myself together.

When the time comes, I board and find my seat. I buckle my belt and then open the bag. I can see the glint of a charm, and I shake the contents of the bag into my hand. There are two charms. The first is a simple palm tree to symbolize our tropical island stay, and the second is a painted heart. My hand closes around it, and I press my fist to my heart, covering it with my other hand.

He gave me a heart. His heart? Why didn't he let me open it in front of him? I have two hours and thirty-five minutes until my flight lands in Houston to think about what it means.

I struggle over the decisions I just made at the gate, ready to throw them all away to run after Adam, when it hits me. All Ally ever wanted was for me to find myself and be happy. She wouldn't have wanted me to ignore my heart and be alone.

When I land, I call him. He won't get my message until he lands, but even if I never speak to him again, even if he doesn't feel the same way, I have to tell him I love him.

"This is Adam. Leave a message."

I choke back the sob that threatens just from hearing his voice again. "Adam, it's Aubrey. I just had to"—I gulp—"tell you I love you."

I tell him I haven't always loved him. In the beginning, I truly thought he was a jerk. It was over our journey together that my feelings for him changed. I explain that what kept me from saying anything was not knowing if he feels anything more for me.

I have a mild panic attack after sending that message. I put myself out there, and I have no way of knowing if I'll even get a response.

I toy with the bracelet on my wrist, my finger smoothing over the red paint of his heart. I stalk my phone, waiting for a response from him, even though I know he's still in the air. My frustration mounts when my flight out of Houston is delayed. I call my parents to let them know, and I drown my misery in a greasy slice of pizza.

My delay ends up being not one but two hours. It kills me when I realize Adam should have landed by now and didn't call me. I'm dejected when I board my flight. I have been on the trip of a lifetime, and I've seen so many amazing things.

I'm unexpectedly angry with Ally. All those years ago, when we made her Better board, she was well enough to travel. She could have taken this trip. Instead, she waited for this concept of being better before she would allow herself to go. What did that get her? Nothing. It got her nothing.

She stayed in California, dreaming of a trip she would never take, right until the end. I have done the same thing. I should have told Adam that I loved him while I had the chance. Instead, I wimped out and left him a voice mail.

Four hours later, I land in Sacramento. I'm tired. I'm hearthurt, and I have to pee so bad when I get off that plane. I'm readjusting the strap on my backpack when a figure steps right in front of me. I try to move around him in search of my parents.

When he moves to block my path again, I look up at him with a glare. I don't know how or why, but Adam is right in front of me. My mouth drops, and I launch myself into his arms.

"How are you here?" I ask against his lips, needing to kiss him as much as I need to ask that question.

With his arms tightly wrapped around me, he pulls his face away to smile down at me. "I take it you're happy to see me."

I nod, smiling. "But how?"

"I changed my flight. Had a stop in Minneapolis, but your flight's delay saved me."

"I was so annoyed with that delay."

"I'll bet." He slowly lowers me to the ground. "Wanna introduce me to your parents now?"

My mouth drops, and I look around until I see them sitting at a coffee kiosk. I tug Adam over toward them while they stand and meet us halfway.

"Mom! Dad! I missed you guys so much," I say, hugging them.

We stand there awkwardly for a moment until my dad says, "And this is Adam?"

"Oh, right. Sorry. Mom, Dad, I'd like you to meet Adam Burke. Adam, this is my mom and dad."

They shake hands, my father clearly appraising him.

I turn to Adam, linking my fingers through his. "Where are you staying? How long are you staying?"

"I know a guy who lives in Rancho Cordova. I thought I'd stay at his place."

I look at my parents, wondering if maybe they'd offer to let Adam stay with us, and then I think better of it. This is clearly happening way too fast for them.

Adam already has his luggage, so we all walk together to get mine. While we wait for it, my mom invites Adam to come back to the house with us, and then after dinner, I can drive him to his friend's house.

When we get to my house, Adam sets up his laptop, so my parents can scroll through all the pictures he took while we go and talk in my backyard.

"What are we doing?" I ask, sinking into my swing.

He sits on the ground in front of me, holding then releasing my feet, as I slowly swing back and forth. "I want to be with you, Aubrey—if you want that too. We just need to figure out where that will be."

"You'd move for me?"

He lifts my captured foot to kiss my ankle. "If that's what it takes."

"Or I could move to New York." I ease off the swing and onto his lap.

"Is that what you'd want?" He loops his arms around my waist.

"You already have a place and a job there. It makes the most sense."

"I don't want to take you away from your home." He tucks a wayward strand of hair behind my ear.

I lean in to kiss him. "You can be my home."

EPILOGUE

Twelve Months Later

"Honey, I'm home," I call out, kicking the door shut behind me, cringing at the boom it makes.

I'm still working on getting our neighbor, Mr. Wiltshire, to like me. He isn't a fan of loud noises.

Adam walks out of the bathroom with a towel wrapped around his waist. I lose my appetite for the takeout I'm carrying, hungry for him instead. I drop it on the counter before pulling his face down to mine for a kiss.

"You naked, me bed," he commands, pulling away to lower our Murphy bed.

Considering the chill in the air, I have lots of layers to deal with. He gets tired of waiting for me, and he starts helping me undress. We tumble onto our bed moments later. The thought still thrills me—our bed, in our apartment.

I moved in with him one week after he met me in Sacramento. My parents adored him and got as used to the idea of me living across the country as they had when they thought I was going to Yale.

Now, I work in a no-kill animal shelter. Adam still loves me even though he makes me shower first on the days I come home smelling like a wet dog. I've also gone back to school. I'm studying to be a veterinarian's assistant. I'm trying to talk Adam into getting a pet. Our place is too small for a dog so I've been hinting at how cute I think the kittens at the shelter are.

I'm also tweeting now. On Adam's account he mainly just posts pictures while I use my one hundred and forty characters to describe the sights I've seen. Together we went through all of Adam's pictures to pick out some shots to frame and add to the walls of our apartment. It was then I realized he somehow captured each moment I said good-bye. Together, we made an album just of those moments for my parents.

When we flew out to visit them it was his gift to them. Funnily, any talk of us rushing stopped shortly afterward. During that trip—through pictures, cards, and old videos—he really got to meet my Ally. We also took a drive with my parents out to the Golden Gate Bridge. There, with my mom and my dad, we scattered the rest of her ashes.

Somehow, it comforts me, knowing that no matter where I go in the world, she's already there.

Adam and I have gone on only one trip overseas since I moved in with him. We went to Moscow. Adam was in heaven while visiting all of the old buildings and churches.

One day, after he slipped into a gift shop, he handed me a bag. I emptied the contents into my palm, expecting to see another charm for my bracelet. An engagement ring tumbled out instead.

We're planning a destination wedding.

The End

CANCER
AND
HARRY POTTER

Better was inspired by my own story.

You wouldn't think cancer would be the first thing someone thinks about when thinking of Harry Potter, but for me, it always will be.

I had not read the book when the first movie came out. It was just before Christmas 2001. At the time, I lived in Phoenix, but I was back home in Alexandria for a visit.

My father was ill, having had a stroke earlier that year. Being home was hard, and seeing him like that was surreal. I had an escape though—my friend, Cameron. Cameron was one of those guys that it took me too long to figure out just how wonderful he was.

We met in seventh grade French class. My mother met his mother the night before, and she made a point of telling me that Cameron and I should be friends.

When I saw him, I disagreed. While he was always handsome, he had a quirky fashion sense that I did not get. It was middle school, and I was trying so hard to fit in. He didn't seem to mind standing out though, and he was always wearing this ridiculous trench coat. We became friends.

To this day, I'm not certain that I have ever known someone as truly sweet and generous as Cameron was. I say *was* because Cameron died. That's where the cancer comes in. I'll get back to that.

At the end of and after high school, I was in an extremely toxic and abusive relationship. During one of our breakups, I went out on a couple of dates with Cameron. Looking back, I wish I had been ready for him, but I wasn't. My head was not in the right place to deal with accepting my attraction to the guy with the mohawk when I was still all messed-up over a guy who was nothing but a thug. Cameron was too different.

I moved away, and when I came back for a visit, we went on another date. He took me to the little Chinese place next to where the Blockbuster was. Over dinner, he told me he had cancer.

He learned this during his freshman year of college. He kept having stomach pains and went twice to the student clinic, only to be sent away with painkillers.

The next time, his mom told him to go to the emergency room. They found a tumor.

I remember being shocked over dinner but not scared. Nobody I knew had died of cancer. He would be fine.

We kept in touch while I was in Arizona, talking on the phone maybe once every couple of months. Just as I suspected, the cancer went away. He beat it. He even went back to school and worked up the nerve to ask some girl out. I was jealous.

He never got a chance to go on that date. The cancer came back, and he moved back home to Virginia.

The next time I saw him was December 2001. He looked different but not bad. We went to see *Harry Potter and the Sorcerer's Stone*. He had already seen it, but he took me anyway.

That was his way, always looking out for me. We swam together during high school. I remember my coach wanted me to join this other team. I was scared because I wouldn't know anyone. Cameron decided to join too.

He looked at me, so serious. "We'll carpool."

And then, through that awful relationship, I remember him putting his hands on either side of my face, trying to convince me I deserved better, wanting to beat up my ex for hurting me.

That December in 2001, I was home one week, and I saw Cameron three times.

I was busy when I first got back to Arizona. I didn't call him right away. When I did, it was just after New Year's. He was in the hospital. I spoke to his younger brother. He told me Cameron overdid it when I was in town. I didn't know.

Cameron called me when he got out of the hospital. It was the first time I actually considered that he might die. I remember saying that he couldn't die, that I was putting my foot down, like I had any power. I made him promise me he wouldn't die, and he did. He promised. When we hung up, I was certain he would beat it again. That was the last time I ever spoke to him.

When my caller ID flashed his name, I answered all happy and excited to talk to him. But it wasn't him. It was his dad.

The second he said, "This is Cameron's dad," I knew.

We didn't talk long, and I honestly don't remember anything after he said, "Cameron is gone."

At the time, I was a smoker. I went out on my front porch to cry and have a smoke. I lived in Phoenix. It never really got windy unless there was a monsoon, which between you and me, I never understood what the big deal was. It was just rain. It rained all the time in Virginia. Either way, it was windy, really windy, and there wasn't a monsoon. It felt like Cameron was coming to say good-bye, using the wind to wipe the tears from my face.

After that night, I began to associate wind with feeling Cameron's presence. I would lie in bed at night and turn the ceiling fan above my bed to the highest setting to imagine it was him. He was the wind.

Harry Potter helped me grieve. It gave me time to rest in my memories of Cameron. I bought each book as they came out and saw each movie.

When the second movie came out, I went by myself on opening weekend. It was packed, standing in line with little kids dressed up as wizards. I had people, strangers really, sitting on either side of me. They probably thought I was off when I sobbed through the opening credits. I just wished Cameron were there with me. That familiar opening melody broke my heart.

By the third movie's release, I had a boyfriend. We were pretty serious, but he understood why I went to that movie alone. I told him about Cameron. When we became engaged, he started to come with me. He would hold my hand while I cried.

The last two movies were hard. The books were all out. The end was in sight. During *Harry Potter and the Deathly Hallows: Part 1*, I came close to inflicting bodily harm on the people sitting behind me who were laughing during that scene at the end with Harry and Dobby on the beach. Didn't they know? Couldn't they understand these movies, this experience, meant so much to me? The last movie was the hardest for me.

I am now married to a wonderful man, and we have beautiful children. I understand how blessed I am. I mourn the what-if with Cameron, and even if nothing had ever come of us, I feel sad every day because the world lost such a beautiful soul.

So, for me, Harry Potter will always make me think of Cameron and the cancer that took him away.

ABOUT THE AUTHOR

Carey Heywood is a self-published *New York Times* and *USA Today* bestselling author with six books out and many more to come.

She was born and raised in Alexandria, Virginia. Ever the mild-mannered citizen, Carey spends her days working in the world of finance, and at night, she retreats into the lives of her fictional characters.

Supporting her all the way are her husband, three sometimes-adorable children, and their nine-pound attack Yorkie.

www.careyheywood.com
www.facebook.com/careyheywoodauthor
www.twitter.com/careylolo

OTHER BOOKS BY
CAREY HEYWOOD

A Bridge of Her Own
Uninvolved
Stages of Grace
Him
Her

ACKNOWLEDGMENTS

Writing is incredibly therapeutic. Before I sat down and wrote about Cameron and what his loss meant to me, I could not even say his name without crying. It might sound silly, but I truly feel as though he helped me write this book. He was my Ally. His kindness and generosity as a friend is his everlasting legacy.

There are many other people who helped me along the way: my betas—Nasha, Judy, Kendall, Evette (Boom), Amy, Michelle, Jennifer, Keren, Kristy, Rebecca, Bobbie, and Mandy; Yesenia Vargas, my editor; Jovana Shirley with Unforeseen Editing; Sarah Hansen of Okay Creations; Toski Covey Photography, for making the picture in my head come to life; Dan Mandel, my agent; Chastity and Donna with RockStarLit; and Nita, for my beautiful book trailers.

My girls—Renee, Jennifer, Lisa, Penny, Helen, Rachel, Gareth (honorary girl title bestowed), Michelle, and Kendall—You are always there for me. Thank you.

My author wife, Melissa Collins—I am thankful for your friendship and support each and every day. You are also totally out of my league, thanks for pretend marrying me and being my happy place when stuff gets scary.

To Jennifer Berg, the only reason I'm not a dill hole is because you are also not a dill hole. I'm pretty sure if you were my inner dill hole would rear its ugly head. I love you, you are my kind of cray cray.

To Lisa Paul, you kill me, seriously. When we're together, even virtually, insane stuff happens. How else can I explain witnessing an actual Swat Team raid? If I ever write a crime drama I blame that phone call.

Thank you to all the readers and blogs who help other readers find out about my books.

Last but by no means ever least, I owe a huge thank you to real life husband and our three kids.

Made in the USA
Middletown, DE
02 January 2017